Hippies
of
Hollywood

Stories from the Sixties

V.M. Brott, M.Ed.

Pearblossom Press

Printed in the United States of America

ISBN-13: 978-0615991122
ISBN-10: 0615991122

Pearblossom Press
Springfield, Illinois

For educator discounts contact publisher
pearblossompressbooks@gmail.com

Clip Art by Microsoft Word

This book is dedicated to
my children and grandchildren.
My family and friends have my heartfelt
gratitude for their encouragement.
Love, V.B.

Contents

Shoes

As an infant I wore slippers

As a toddler I wore sturdy supportive leather shoes

As a preteen I wore flip flops

As a teenager I wore pointed high heels

*As a young woman of the sixties, I wore bracelets on my ankles
and rings on my toes,
Barefooted and independently free*

As a working woman I wore pointed high heels

As an older mom I wore flip flops

As a grandmother I wore sturdy supportive leather shoes

As a retired grandmother I wear slippers

2. An Introduction -- Hello Hollywood

The hippie generation burst forth like an explosion of social revolution! During the 1960s, there were no cell phones, computers, or car seat belts. You could not vote until age 21, gas was 25 cents a gallon, minimum wage was about $2.00 an hour, and a cheap hotel room was $5.00 a night.

As a young adult, I wanted excitement away from a humdrum life and existence. I was idealistic and yearned for people who were genuine and resisted a materialistic lifestyle. I met some friends who introduced me to Hollywood; I was 19 years old. I knew I would be back many times again and again.

Hollywood was crowded with tourists and locals alike, it was a wonderful, welcoming world of excitement, fun, noise and friendly people. Hollywood gave you a sense of freedom.

The Sunset Strip was a popular place filled with young people, tourists and the wealthy. Sometimes it became so thick with crowds that police cruisers would use bull horns to order everyone to "DISPERSE! DISPERSE!

11

DISPERSE!" The young people defiantly ignored them, and the cops seemed frustrated.

I thought the hippies of Hollywood seemed fun and exciting. What exactly was a hippie? I'm not sure anyone could give an accurate description, or agree on one.

Hippies were generally free thinkers and nonconformists. World peace, freedom, and brotherly love were their highest ideals. They have been stereotyped as people who indulged in "sex, drugs and rock and roll." However, many did not use drugs and had faithful relationships, often leading to marriage.

The hippies of Hollywood during the late 1960s consisted of a variety of people. Some were young adults who were conservative at home and work, but escaped and let loose on weekends. They were weekend hippies.

My generation may be remembered as all mixed up in a kind of madness gone wild, but in some ways we were more innocent than today's generation.

Read on, if you dare, if you care, but most of all be loved, be blessed dear reader.

Welcome to the 1960s!

3. Santa Ana Winds

Hot dry desert winds occasionally sweep through the valleys across southern California. Known as the "Santa Ana Winds," they will ravish your hair and flutter your clothing like a flag in the wind. Invigorating, they draw you in their direction. Captivated, you surrender to their warmth.

Sometimes they are called the hot breath of "Satana." Legends claim the devil winds ignite wild fires and provoke emotions.

I may have encountered Satan himself in a parking lot in the city of Santa Ana when the moon was full and the hot winds were blowing. I eluded him, maybe with the help of Saint Ann herself.

My family moved to Southern California when I was eighteen. I met some kids in a psychedelic shop; it was during the 1960's. Just a naïve girl from the Midwest, I was undergoing culture shock. Orange County seemed cold and unfriendly.

It was really nice to have some friends. The little shop was fragrant with the scent of jasmine and sandalwood incense. A room in back was decorated by posters; black lights illuminated their bright colors.

My new friends welcomed me. Mostly young misfits, they jokingly called themselves "Sgt. Pepper's Lonely Hearts Club Band" referring to the song by the Beatles.*

"THE ESTABLISHMENT" was to be resisted; rebelling against it was encouraged. Timothy Leary was telling the counterculture of the time to "Tune-in, turn-on and drop-out."

Some of my friends hated cops. They told me they harassed people for having long hair, and even jailed a guy in Newport Beach for using the flag for a seat cover in his car. Cops were never to be trusted.

I felt accepted by the friendly group, by everyone except Lori. She thought of me as a "goodie-goodie." I wanted to be friends, so when she invited me for a visit, I accepted.

I never made it. I'm not sure the address even existed. Thinking back, that night still gives me the creeps.

The neighborhood was in an older part of Santa Ana. I was pretty and young, but naïve in the way I thought I was cool. Like many teens, I believed nothing bad would happen to me. I knew all there was to know. I got out of my car and was locking it, when a police car rolled up.

"Hello, Miss. May I ask you what you're doing?" A balding, old cop flashed his bright light across me. Humiliated, I felt like a victim of the "hassling" I heard so much about.

*"Sgt. Pepper's Lonely Hearts Club Band," The Beatles, 1967

I stood up straight and answered boldly: "Did I do something wrong?"

"Well, no. I'm more concerned about *something wrong* happening to *you*."

"Don't worry about me. I'm fine. I'm visiting a friend." I retorted.

"Alright, but let me warn you, this area is not safe."

As defiant as a cat, I turned away and muttered: "I hate cops."

After he left, I resumed looking for the house. Walking around a corner, I began roaming and soon became lost. I found myself in a large parking lot and alley behind several apartment buildings. The wind carried an array of distant noises, TV's, music, barking dogs, and the usual.

Suddenly, a gush of wind brought the stench of garbage from the overflowing dumpsters. It seemed to alert me that something more foul was lurking in the dark shadows.

That's when I noticed a man wearing a white tee shirt was sitting on an upstairs balcony facing my direction. Was he watching me? A little fearful, I decided to give up my search, find my car and get out of there.

I held a whistle in my hand. I thought it would attract attention if anyone bothered me. I headed for the way out, back to the street, when I was abruptly startled. A man dressed in black stood behind me, very close, not a foot away.

He was short, but muscular with slick black hair. His eyes were dark liquid pools reflecting the dim lights surrounding the alley way.

15

He breathed heavily; his nostrils flared. His eyes devoured each part of me, drinking in all that he saw. With hands gloved in black leather, he gripped my shoulders.

Drawing closer like a panther with its prey, he was ready to strike, to swoop down like death all in black.

"Come here. Closer to me!" He grabbed my arm firmly. His seductive, yet threatening commands were heavily accented. His fiery breath felt hot on my neck. He held something metal that flashed in the moon light.

I tried to act calm like you do around barking dogs, but my reaction was more like a deer facing the headlights of an oncoming truck. I was so filled with terror I could barely move.

With a trembling hand, I clutched the whistle. He quickly spotted it, tensed, and then laughed when he realized what it was. I had neither breath nor courage to do anything with it. Grinning, he lifted a strand of my hair. Shaking, I dropped the worthless whistle.

If ever I faced Satan, it was on that night with the hot winds of Santa Ana blowing. I glanced around nervously, seeking the man in the tee shirt on the second floor balcony – the man who had faced me, the man I had initially feared – hoping now he was still watching and would help.

Frantically scanning the balconies, I searched them, but my eyes could not focus from my fright. I blinked tightly, and then spotted the balcony where he had been. There was only an empty chair.

I felt doomed as my assailant held my arms, his body like a black cape enveloping me from my escape and melting my strength into frozen fear. I was a rabbit in the jaws of a creature of the night. I wanted to run, but was too afraid. Where was the guy from the balcony? With my luck, he probably went inside for the rest of the night.

Suddenly someone shouted in Spanish. It was a man's voice, persistent, calling to the man in black. Maybe he had an enemy, or owed someone money. Possibly, it was the man from the balcony trying to rescue me.

I knew the conflict was enough to distract him and weaken his grip. I seized the opportunity and dashed quickly away from him.

He shouted to the other man. An argument erupted. I began running with a good start. But all too soon, I heard footsteps dashing in my direction. I quickly turned the corner.

Sweat began to cover my face. In a panic, I couldn't remember where I parked my car, or even what my car looked like. I couldn't think straight.

Panting like a hunted animal, my heart beat rapidly, my legs trembled as I ran. The warm wind dashed at my back, hurrying me on.

I raced up the stairs onto the porch of an old house with lights on inside. Desperately, I pounded on the door. I heard the voice of an old man murmur from within.

"Who's there?" He was gruff and suspicious.

I gasped for breath, unable to speak. My delay frightened him, but I was relieved to hear his words in English. He would understand me. I knocked again.

"What do you want?"

Finally forcing myself to speak, my voice quivered. I begged: "Please help me, someone is chasing me."

The old man was sympathetic, but afraid:

"I can't let you in, I'm sorry."

I looked around frantically. "Just call the police. Please!" My voice was low and shaking, but he understood.

"I'll call, but I won't open the door."

"I'll hide on your porch; keep the lights off so he doesn't see me." I threw myself down behind the porch enclosure, near a few large potted plants. I could smell the soil and foliage.

Clinging to a heavy planter with desperate need for comfort and protection, I lay still, trying to control my panting. He might hear it. I forced myself to be still. I sensed the old man was waiting just as silently within.

Then, the wind stopped. I could hear the sound of footsteps, walking briskly, slowing now and then. They approached the house and came nearly to a stop. I trembled. He sounded close. My heart throbbed, anticipating what might happen next. I dared not take a breath.

Suddenly the silence was broken by his heavy shoes rapidly pounding pavement; growing fainter in the distance until they were lost in the night. Sweat covered my neck; I felt it trickling down my back, soaking my long hair.

"You're safe now." The old man tapped on the window glass, smiling proudly. I looked out into the night; it was as though an evil shadow had been swept away by the wind.

I could now see the old gentleman clearly behind the lace curtains. He was hunched over, and frail. With a crippled hand trembling from age, he pointed to a police car approaching slowly. The same balding old cop who spoke to me earlier aimed a bright spot light along the sidewalks, illuminating the entire neighborhood. His patrol car must have frightened the creep who frightened me.

Regaining composure, I stood and faced the elderly man. His worn expression brightened with a proud smile. Like a knight in shining armor, he saved a young lady in distress. His moist eyes sparkled like blue diamonds.

"Thank you." With youthful fingertips, I gratefully tapped the glass that separated us. He tapped back, nodding kindly, grandfatherly.

I spotted my car a few houses down. Acting as cool as I could, as if nothing had happened, I left the porch. With all the arrogance and innocence of youth, I got into my car, and drove away. In my rear view mirror, I saw the squad car continue its search in the area.

Turning onto a main street, I gladly left that neighborhood. With a sudden surge of energy, I opened the windows and sped up.

While the wind dried the sweat from my face it danced through the dampened strands of my hair, replenishing my soul.

I never said I hated cops again.

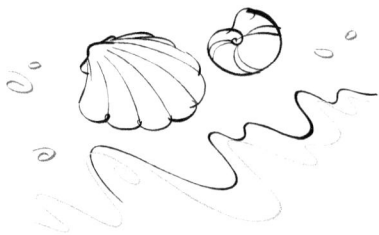

4. The Doors

Cindy invited me to a party at Laguna Beach. I loved the quaint little tourist town. Exploring the tide pools at Crescent Bay was fascinating. When the tides were low, it was like a door opened to reveal the mysteries of the ocean. I often thought life itself is like a tide pool filled with mysteries.

The party was for some guy, that's all she told me. I think his mom was a friend of her mom's. They wanted to invite as many kids as possible, especially pretty girls.

I guess he didn't have any friends. Maybe they were visitors from out of town, who knows?

We parked on Pacific Coast Highway in a business district, walked behind some buildings and up, up a long stair case to a little beach house. I assumed it was a rental, but didn't know for sure. It was daylight when we arrived, but it soon grew dark.

The mom opened the door and invited us in. We were offered food and the stereo was playing popular music. Candles were lit around the small living room, hippie style. Most of us sat on the floor.

Although the atmosphere was youthful, it was more of an adult party. Regardless how they tried to make it seem cool, it had older people written all over it.

They wanted to make us feel welcome, but I felt like a prop in a movie. Whenever I asked Cindy a question about the party, she would reply, "I don't know." Then she would stand up and disappear for a while. I got the idea she was avoiding my questions.

I asked another girl about the boy. I could only gather that it was his eighteenth birthday.

"Where is he, why isn't he out here enjoying the party?"

"I think he's in the other room." She replied flatly and motioned toward a short hallway.

"Why?" I glanced over and noticed his door was closed.

"No one seems to know. Go ask his mom."

I didn't want to ask his mom. There was something nervous and fidgety about her, as though she had a lot on her mind. Besides, she was surrounded by the older people and they made me feel like a kid.

Finally, she placed a birthday cake on the coffee table in the middle of the room and lit candles. We all sang "Happy Birthday" to the cake, but the boy was nowhere around. As his mom removed the candles, her hand seemed to be shaking.

"Why doesn't your son come out and enjoy his party?"

She looked at me with an expression that told me she dreaded the question. Her eyes were bloodshot, as though she had been crying. I wondered why she would cry during a birthday celebration.

"Oh, he just wants to enjoy the party from his room." Her response was like a fake cover up.

"But his door is closed," I responded.

She smiled nervously. "Yes, but he can still hear all the party sounds."

My puzzled expression begged an explanation, and so she continued. "Would you like to meet him?" She spoke quickly, I nodded.

"He's asking each guest to visit one at a time. I'll let you know when he's ready."

She smiled briefly and then abruptly left. It was apparent she didn't want to hear any more questions from me.

The party began to drag on; the food was eaten, and the music was growing stale. Cindy sat down on the floor next to me.

"We're here for my mom. Just hang in there. We'll leave soon." She spoke apologetically, but I had become curious about the boy and was looking forward to meeting him.

I watched as each guest walked through that mysterious door to see him. They came out breathing and alive, so it couldn't have been that bad. Then it was my turn.

His mother moved toward me, gently tapped my arm and quietly requested I visit her son. She walked me to the door and gestured for me to enter.

I approached the young man who sat on a single bed.

He was wearing pajamas with a wrinkled robe. A thin blanket was loosely draped over some contraption nearby. As I stood before him, I could tell by his smile he was pleased with my appearance.

Suddenly he turned to his mother, who was still standing inside the door. He gruffly shouted at her: "DON'T JUST STAND THERE, CLOSE THE DOOR AND GET OUT!"

"If you need anything, just call. I'll be just outside the door." She addressed me, but I sensed she meant the words for both of us. The young man picked up his slipper, and angrily threw it at the door as it closed. I stood before him with a solemn look.

"Never mind her. Long story. Don't ask." He said sheepishly. I gave him a half smile.

He thanked me for attending the party and said I was the best looking girl there.

"Sit down, please." He motioned to a pile of pillows on the other side of a small table which separated the two of us. A record player was placed close enough to the bed for him to operate it.

I sat on the pillows, hippie style. We exchanged smiles. He was good looking, but thin, pale, with red rims around his eyes and dark circles beneath them. It was clear he was sickly. Now, I understood why he didn't join the party.

My eyes curiously drifted to the mysterious thin blanket covering some contraption. He noticed and shoved his arm against it. "Don't mind this crap. Don't even look at it. I hate all of it!"

Frustrated, he grabbed an album from a pile on the table, removed the record from its jacket, and placed it on the turntable.

"Do you like *The Doors*?"

"Sure, I love their music!"

"Can you answer a question for me?"

"I'll try."

"I've been asking everyone, but nobody can give me a good answer." He sounded frustrated, irritated.

The record began playing while Jim Morrison sang his famous recording, "The End." *

"Hear that? Morrison says the end is a friend, but that doesn't make sense to me. Like, when somebody dies, it's the end for that person. So, how can it be a friend?"

I thought he was being poetic, seeking some deeper meaning, but his intense stare directly into my eyes told me he was desperate for a convincing answer. I wanted to help him, but didn't know what to say. The record played on.

"I always looked forward to turning 18, but it's no big deal." He seemed to be holding back emotions, struggling with his words. With reddened eyes fastened on mine, he blurted: "Death is not a friend!"

Too young to have the answers he craved, I sat stone faced. He needed strength. Sympathy and his mother's tears made him angry. I had to figure out how the end could be a friend. Jim Morrison claimed it was, but he wasn't there to explain the lyrics.

There I sat, nineteen years old. What did I know? My brain searched the database within my memory. I remembered my grandmother.

"Well, death can be a friend if life is difficult in this

*"The End," by Jim Morrison, The *Doors*, 1967.

world. It can be a passage to a better place."

He stared at me with interest. I tried my best to help him, hoping I wouldn't make things worse.

"You see, my grandmother had been suffering from a terrible illness. For her, the end was a friend who came to take her to a beautiful paradise, a world of happiness.

He listened closely to every word I said. When the song ended, we just gazed at each other. Then he spoke.

"I never thought of it that way, but you're right. The end can be a friend."

"When one door closes, another door opens!" I added. He contemplated the idea, then smiled and nodded.

Before the next song began, the boy clutched his arms over his chest and with a grimace, drew his legs up and fell back onto the bed, loudly gasping for breath.

The door quickly flung open. His mother came rushing in to help. I saw her strength this time, like an angel of mercy. She exposed a kind of oxygen tank from beneath the thin blanket. She motioned for me to leave.

"He'll be alright, go back to the party. Everything is O.K."

I closed the door and left the room and its mysteries. Although a little frazzled, I joined the others. Cindy sat silently, eyes closed, apparently lost in the sounds of the stereo.

After the boy's mother returned to speak to the other adults, it was apparent the party was over. Cindy left the room to gather our coats. While she was gone, the boy's mom approached me. She seemed calmer, more uplifted than she had been earlier.

"My son wanted me to tell you thank you for him."
She warmly held my hand.

"For what?" I asked.

"He didn't say exactly, but I think it was something
you told him. Whatever it was, you made him happy."

She smiled warmly and added: "I want to thank you,
too." Her eyes sparkled like stars in a night sky.

Out the door, Cindy and I left. We descended down,
down those long stairs and back to Pacific Coast Highway.
Rushing traffic passed indifferently.

The sun was setting over Laguna Beach. I could hear
the evening surf roll in along the shore. I imagined it
covering the tide pools and their mysteries.

A slight breeze swept my cheek. It seemed to carry
my whispered "good-bye" up, up to a boy who waited
within the sunset of a cloudless sky.

Tomorrow I would have to be at work at
9 a.m. For me, life would go on as usual.

5. The Jimi Hendrix Experience

What I would experience that September evening in 1968 was way beyond my expectations! While working for the phone company in Santa Ana, California, Cindy and I became good friends. She was hip, and I liked hanging out with her.

Her older brother gave her two tickets to the Jimi Hendrix Experience at the Hollywood Bowl. He had to cancel his plans at the last minute. She invited me, and I accepted.

Cindy knew about all the cool stuff and what was popular. I never heard of Jimi Hendrix, but that didn't surprise her. I had nothing else to do. Besides, I saw pictures of the Hollywood Bowl on post cards, and I was a little curious about it.

That evening was beautiful. We arrived early and found our seats; they were high up and far in back. Cindy was a little disappointed, but it would be a good concert anyway.

Strong winds had been blowing through the distant canyons, igniting wild fires the past few days. Warm breezes swept through the outdoor amphitheater carrying a sweet smoky scent of burnt wood. The atmosphere was ethereal, electrical, and exuberant.

Far below, the stage was illuminated and set beneath a band shell constructed of concentric arches. Directly in front of the stage was a pool of water, similar to a swimming pool.

It was called the Hollywood Bowl because the amphitheater seating had been carved into a concave shape on the hillside facing the stage. The "bowl" design created wonderful acoustics.

Cindy explained that Jimi Hendrix was a unique electric guitar player, and the sounds I was about to hear were unlike any produced by other musicians. I couldn't imagine what she was talking about.

She told me, "Just wait, you'll see!"

The seating area was surrounded by fencing, but a few people found a way in without a ticket. They nervously rushed past us, and then tried to seem inconspicuous.

No one in the audience seemed to care, but soon security arrived. We watched as a few guys were taken away. A guard was then stationed at the fence.

More people arrived and found their seats. It was exciting to be part of this event. I could sense it would be something special.

The audience included all young hippie types. Cindy and I blended well with them. We wore long straight hair, flair pants, colorful blouses with hues of purple, fringed suede purses, knee high boots, and Indian beads.

She wore a brass peace symbol; I wore an ankh, an ancient Egyptian symbol for eternal life. We were definitely hip enough to be accepted in the crowd.

When the concert began, people became excited, almost to frenzy. Cindy was right about his music, it was amazing.

Hendrix had the ability to maneuver his guitar to make it "sing" the heartfelt emotions that seemed to explode within his soul, transpire through his fingertips, and explode onto the strings of his guitar.

Electrified, it came to life; its unique sounds lifted the emotions of the audience to a higher level. Our spirits joined with the musical notes to dance throughout the amphitheater.

Reflected by the pool of water, sound waves reverberated at the curvature where the audience was sitting. Striking each of us, they caught up our excitement, bounced back to Hendrix and created a kind of musical rapture that united us all.

No audio recording could compare to being physically present to experience the otherworldly resonance of the sounds produced by Hendrix and his guitar.

While he performed, the audience lost control. People couldn't stay seated, they jumped up, danced where they stood or in the aisles. They seemed overcome with euphoria.

Our views became blocked by the chaos. Cindy and I couldn't see Hendrix very well, but we noticed that someone jumped into the pool of water in front of the stage to be closer to him and his music.

Soon afterwards, others rushed out of their seats toward the stage and began dancing. Then a few more people jumped into the pool. It was crazy!

The microphone was seized by someone in charge and the audience was sternly warned about the danger of electrocution in the pool. Water was being splashed on the stage and could injure the musicians.

Some people ignored the warnings as if they hadn't heard them. Cindy and I watched, stunned by the actions of the fans.

Yet, a wild and wonderful feeling spread throughout the crowd, filling the night air with life and excitement. We were like one body, all part of a whole.

We sensed our strength as we watched security scurry about in an attempt to keep the concert orderly. There was a kind of power we felt when united. We were the baby boomer generation and could not be ignored.

After leaving, Cindy and I talked about the music. My favorite was when Hendrix played "The Star Spangled Banner" * on his guitar. It was indescribable.

Listening to his rendition, I felt patriotic and proud of my country. Without words, he was able to express the feelings and yearnings of my generation.

When the music reached the part that would say: "the rocket's red glare, the bombs bursting in air," * it was as if you could hear the missiles, bombs and voices crying out, reflecting war and all its horrors.

*"Star Spangled Banner" *Rainbow Bridge* Album by Jimi Hendrix, released 1971.
*"Star Spangled Banner" lyrics by Francis Scott Key, 1814.

The great ideals of our Nation seemed intermingled with distortions; to me, this was symbolized in the version Hendrix played.

My generation yearned for a world without war, one in which mankind would love one another and respect the earth and all living things.

At least, that's what I thought.

Nevertheless, I was gradually being introduced to a new outlook, and I was drawn to it like a moth to fire!

EARTH'S MOON

6. Moon Light at Griffith Park

Have you ever observed the night sky and wondered if someone may be watching you from above? Griffith Park is known for its wonderful observatory. From there you can look at the moon and stars until you realize just how small and insignificant we seem in this large vast space of a universe.

The park has an elevation of over 1000 ft. and overlooks Los Angeles, California. It consists of a few thousand acres and is nestled in a hilly region with plenty of room for hiking and enjoying the outdoors.

During the late sixties, young adults met at the park for what were called "Love-ins." All sorts of people would show up: flower children, bikers, Hare Krishna devotees, hippies, political radicals, and the curious. The park was large enough for everyone to scatter about in groups. People were generally friendly, non-judgmental, and accepting of one another.

Strolling through the park, you could experience a multiplicity of atmospheres. Guitars, flutes, tambourines, junk bands and radios were heard in every direction, and sometimes the sounds blended.

All one had to do was find a place to sit on the ground, and join in. You were instantly accepted and often treated like an old friend. No one felt lonely, inferior, or unaccepted.

The concept of brotherly love was enjoyed by all. Although on a few occasions, a disruption among the bikers would emerge, but it was always contained within their group.

To my knowledge, they never went looking for trouble and everyone else just steered clear of them. They were always dominant. Lining up their "hogs" in a row in the parking lot signified their presence. No one dared get within twenty feet of those magnificent Harleys.

The cops would cruise the area more frequently when the bikers were present, but they remained within the law and ignored them. I marveled at their lack of fear of what was referred to as "the badged intruders."

One Sunday, I drove with some friends to the park because we had nothing else to do. I was sitting on the grass near the carousel, enjoying the music and sounds of the children playing when a young man sat down next to me.

He was attractive and friendly. His hair was neatly cut, not long, and he was clean shaven, dressed nicely, and spoke with an accent. He said he was a college student on break and was visiting a relative.

We walked through the park and enjoyed casual small talk. He was very respectful and a real gentleman. When it was time to leave, he kissed me.

"I've enjoyed meeting you. Will you be here again next Sunday?"

"I may have to work." I explained.

"Well, get the day off and let's meet here again."

"If I can't make it next Sunday, I will see you the following Sunday." I promised. He seemed alright with that. We did not exchange phone numbers. We would meet again at the carousel area. Mom and Dad would be happy I met a well-mannered, nice college student.

When I asked if anyone would change schedules with me at work, no one could. I missed meeting him that Sunday, but was anxious for the next.

No love-in was held on that particular day and my friends weren't interested in going. I decided to drive to the park by myself. I arrived at exactly the time we had agreed upon and sat near the carousel as planned. There were fewer people than usual.

He did not arrive on time; in fact I sat there almost an hour. I became bored and was thinking of driving home.

Suddenly a pair of aggressive hands gripped my eyes from behind, it was a childish game of guess who, but the grip was prolonged and forceful.

It frightened me because I didn't know who it was. I didn't struggle but remained still, aware that many families were around. I felt safe for the most part.

Finally, he released his grip and sat down next to me. His attitude was different, annoyed, agitated.

"I've been watching you for a while. How do you like waiting for someone who didn't show up?" He referred to the previous Sunday.

"Don't you remember? I told you I might not be able to get that day off."

"Did you even try? I'm sure someone would have traded." He was sarcastic, critical.

"Yes, of course I tried."

"Well, you couldn't have tried very hard."

"I did. Don't be mad. I really wanted to see you again, and here we are. Let's enjoy the day."

He seemed to accept that, but he wasn't quite the same as he was before. He spoke very quickly and seemed somewhat nervous. Sometimes he didn't make sense.

"Do you think the trees are aware of us? I heard they are conscious of what people are doing, but are helpless to stop them. Do you think that's true?"

"I suppose anything is possible." I was cordial, but he began to annoy me. This guy was acting weird. So much for meeting a nice clean cut college guy! This one wasn't a prize.

I noticed my necklace had dropped somewhere.

"Oh, no! I've lost my necklace."

"Well let's look for it. It should be somewhere around where we walked. I'll help you find it."

The necklace had a large turquoise medallion and would be easy to spot. We began to retrace our steps, but people were beginning to leave and dusk was creeping across the sky.

"Just forget it. We better go. People are leaving."

"Good, now it will be easier to find your necklace."

"No, forget it." I began to head back to the parking lot. He gently took my hand.

"Please, let me help. I know we can find it."

"But, it's getting dark."

"Then let's hurry." Quickly, he took me further from the parking lot. Although we were still out in the open, all the people had left the park.

Dusk had come rapidly and left; the darkness of night now arrived and the sun had completely set. The lights came on near the restrooms.

"It's dark! Forget the necklace; I don't care about it anymore. I want to leave." I had no desire to see this guy again. He had been holding my hand firmly, and he pulled me roughly.

"Let's look by the restrooms, there's light over there." He guided me to the area. "Don't worry about the dark."

At this point, I was becoming frightened by his erratic behavior and hoped someone would come out of the restroom, but they were locked. He spoke rapidly, too rapidly. His breathing became heavy.

"We weren't even over here," I protested. He would not let go of my wrists, and tried to convince me he was being helpful, I pulled away, but he held me tightly.

"Let go of me!" I demanded. "I just want to leave."

The moon was bright now. It was a large full moon in a clear sky, lighting the area enough to cast shadows. I tried to wrestle my wrists free from his grip.

"You're not going anywhere." He grabbed both my arms now and would not allow me to leave. I looked around, hoping someone was close by, a park maintenance person, anyone.

"Someone is nearby and watching! You'd better let me go. I'll scream if you don't."

"No one is watching. No one would hear you scream."

"Yes, somewhere, someone can see us. I know it." I protested.

"No one can see or hear us, we are all alone. It's just us and the trees!' He was smug.

Hurriedly directing me to a particular area, he then suddenly pulled me to another. I was confused with his actions. I tried to get away from him, but he was too strong and forceful.

"What are you trying to do?" I was angry, but bewildered by his behavior.

As he held my arms, he appeared troubled as though he was fighting himself. Muttering, his speech became inaudible, his eyes fluttered. He seemed tortured by some demon that possessed him.

Although he held me firmly, something greater held him. I watched his expression contort with inner torment. Still gripping my arms tightly, he looked around anxiously, scoping the area. His intentions were never clear, he acted totally insane, but oddly I remained calm.

His face became a silhouette as the light of the moon beyond grew brighter. His shadow seemed frantic. It was as though good and evil were at war within his soul, or reason was battling with insanity.

While I fiercely twisted to free my arms, I watched his shadow outlined by the moon behind him. I imagined fiery sparks darting from his head as he struggled for self-control.

The moonlight beyond him caught my attention. Its

light was so bright and powerful. I thought of heavenly light and prayed. Maybe it was the altitude with its closer proximity to the sky, or it could have been my imagination, but I like to think of it as "divine intervention."

At that instant, the moon appeared to become larger and brighter than I had ever seen it before. It illuminated us in the surrounding darkness as though we were on stage under a bright spot light.

Just at that moment, a deep voice from the dark hills beyond shouted: "Hey, what's going on over there?"

A man yelled at us from a few hundred feet away. There appeared to be a small group. Another man shouted a loud threat. They sensed foul play and weren't going to let it happen.

Huge dogs accompanied them on leashes. Their barks were powerful, wild with excitement, as if they knew more than the men who led them. They were eager to attack and their threatening primitive calls warned that they could rip apart flesh if set free.

The once dominant little man was now frightened; the tables were turned. He quickly released his grip, flinging me to the ground. Stumbling as he ran off, he raced to his car to escape.

"Hey! We can see you. Stop!" they shouted in turn.

Although their voices grew louder, they were still at a significant distance. I could see them quickly approaching.

"Are you alright?" They called to me. They were running and sounded out of breath.

"Yes, thank you, THANK YOU!" Each time I said it the words became bolder and stronger.

"Did he hurt you? What was he trying to do?"

"I don't know. I'm OK." I was on my feet and began to run.

 You want us to get him?" They asked, but I didn't answer. They had no cars, and cell phones didn't exist. Besides, I had no idea who they were and I had no interest in finding out

I became very angry now, my mind racing, I ran as fast as I could toward my car, in the same direction taken by the little man with the accent. He dared not stop. He was outnumbered by men who could take him down.

I watched him get into his car and I quickly got into mine. I felt like running the coward down. Both in our cars, the playing field would be even. Racing with adrenaline, I followed him in my car toward the entrance to the Golden State Freeway.

He drove in a panic, his car swaying unsteadily. I hoped he would crash. My powerful Ford could easily destroy the rear engine of his little foreign car, sending them both flying into the dark hills. Now, I felt a sense of power over him. It was my turn, and he knew it.

He entered the onramp toward Hollywood, so did I. He hoped to lose me, but I kept my Ford close on his bumper and nudged it a few times.

There were no other cars nearby. He shifted gears several times trying to get his sluggish little car to outrun mine, but it didn't have the power.

I wanted to let my sturdy solid 1954 Ford smash him from behind, jolt his car and send him reeling out of control; but my better judgment restrained me from going further.

Through his back window I could see his silhouette bouncing with panic as his little car struggled. I watched him glance nervously into his rear view mirrors. He frantically pumped the gas pedal forcing his little car to top speed as smoke bellowed from it.

Although I did no damage to him or his car, I grinned complacently as he desperately attempted to escape my wrath. I wanted revenge, but hadn't lost my senses to do anything foolish. I maintained the speed limit, and his car didn't have much power.

As we approached Hollywood, traffic became heavy and safety was an issue. I wasn't going to risk an accident. I ended my pursuit. To his great joy and relief, his car soon blended within traffic. In an instant, he was lost from my view. I hoped I scared him enough to never try that again, but I will never know.

One thing I do know, he was wrong about no one being able to see or hear us. Somebody had been watching, someone with a lot of power, enough to produce a brighter moon.

I knew just who to thank, and I did.

7. Richard the Rogue

He stood tall and proud on the corner of Sunset and Vine. His long hair was combed over his forehead, nearly covering his deep brown eyes.

He had the sparse blonde mustache of a young man. Unlike a lot of hippie guys, he presented himself well. In appearance he had a cute baby-face, like the lead singer from "Herman's Hermits," yet a rough and rugged look like Mick Jagger.

His dark brown eyes captivated me. I felt comfortable and safe with him. He seemed just right, familiar somehow, as if I had known him in another lifetime.

He wore a wide thick leather belt with a large round brass buckle reminiscent of a belt worn by a pirate or a "swash buckler" from an old movie. I could imagine a sword by his side.

With an attitude that was bold and brazen, he held his head high; ready for anything that might come his way.

Richard was street wise, a rogue, and a survivor. He was courageous, but if provoked, he could come across as a little crazy and unpredictable. You didn't mess with him.

Once when threatened, he removed his belt and waved it overhead like a weapon, discouraging a few aggressive challengers who decided to walk away. He knew that large brass buckle could crack open more than one head at a time.

Waving his belt above his head like a mythical hero ready to strike, with both the buckle and his wild eyes flashing in the moonlight, he could frighten his opponents even when outnumbered.

Sometimes he wore two thick sweaters to appear to have a larger build. Steel toed army combat boots were his choice for footwear, never mind the moccasins or sandals worn by flower children. He wore them for protection and knew how to kick if driven to it.

No pretty colored scarves or flowery shirts for Richard, but he wore a few steel rings to reinforce his punches if he needed to use his large fists in a fight. These were the only weapons Richard had available.

He had no interest in breaking the law or going to jail. If police harassed him, he would always cooperate and answer politely, addressing them as "sir." He knew when to walk, and never had to run.

I never saw him fight anyone. I suspected his appearance and actions may have been an act, but regardless, they worked.

Richard seldom spoke of his childhood, and I suspected he wanted to forget it. He did admit that he often ran away as a young teenager, and lived on his own for the past few years.

He travelled across the country's highways, byways, and city streets; his experiences kept him wary, jumpy, and distrustful. He mostly harbored fears of losing his freedom, but he sometimes tempted fate and had no fear of death.

He always tried to make a good impression and present himself well. When I first met him, his "apartment" was nothing more than a dingy room at the Roxy Hotel, just as other hippies at the time.

Although he lacked a college education, he had plenty of life's experiences to earn him a degree at the School of Hard Knocks.

All his possessions were not much more than a few sets of clothes and a shoe box full of treasured trinkets. His transportation was simply his legs and hitchhiking thumb.

Yet, being the naïve young girl I was at barely age twenty, I liked him.

Needless to say, adventures would follow.

8. The Draft Dodger

Richard was a draft dodger, like so many other guys who resisted the draft. Not old enough to vote at 18, many were drafted to fight in a war they didn't support.

One day, Richard returned to the Roxy Hotel, where he had been temporarily staying. The desk clerk was not as friendly as usual. Although he couldn't understand her attitude at the moment, he would later.

In those days, the only televisions in many hotels were located in the lobbies. Richard enjoyed lounging there, in between moments of adjusting the rabbit ears (before cable). Sometimes, he would talk freely with other hotel guests.

Apparently, someone found out he was running from the draft. Draft dodgers were wanted by the F.B.I. and could serve two years in jail. It was reported to the desk clerk that Richard was wanted by the F.B.I., but the person gave no reason. The clerk became watchful.

"Where are you going in such a hurry?" One of Richard's friends asked him after he checked out of the hotel. Richard didn't notice the desk clerk was listening closely.

"Orange, California. Do you know anything about the area?"

"It's very conservative," he commented.

Richard waited for me outside the hotel where I was planning to meet him. The clerk was watching for my car. She jotted down my license plate numbers.

I didn't know Richard was a draft dodger, but he did say he had no interest in the Army.

While driving, the radio was playing. When the news was broadcast, it reported an escalation of troops being sent to Vietnam.

On another station, Country Joe McDonald was singing an anti-war song, one of many that were popular at the time.

"You girls are lucky; you don't have to worry about getting drafted." Richard lamented.

"Yeah, that's true." I agreed. "I know a lot of guys who didn't come back from the war, and those who did aren't always treated with the respect they deserve for all they've been through."

"I don't understand any of it." Richard replied.

"Neither do I. My brother and cousins are serving in the military, but I know others who are avoiding the draft by going to college, claiming they're gay, gaining lots of weight, or even moving to Canada."

"Well, none of that applies to me."

"Some people just say they are conscientious objectors."

Richard grunted, and then changed the subject.

Orange was a quiet place during the late 1960s, especially with their "plaza square" which was actually a little park in the shape of a circle in the middle of town. Small shops in vintage buildings lined the street that curved around the park.

Driving my Ford around the circle, I didn't notice anything unusual, but Richard did.

"Hey, I think we're surrounded by cops."

"No, we're not. I don't see any police cars."

"They're in plain clothes and unmarked cars; they're all around us." Richard observed.

"Why would they be?" I've been driving safely."

While looking around, I missed the turn off and had to drive around the circle a second time.

Richard scanned the road nervously. "There's one behind us, and now one is driving in front of us. There's one in the other lane now, and a few more. They're everywhere!"

As I drove around the circle a third time, I noticed none of the cars turned off. It was like we were all kids on a merry-go-round.

"How do you know they're cops?" I was now beginning to believe him as I saw stern faces staring at us.

"The cars they're driving, the way they look, and the suits they're wearing. They're cops for sure!"

Just when I was about to turn out of the circle, flashing lights from unmarked police cars forced me to pull over and stop. They immediately approached the passenger side and pulled Richard out, escorting him away from me.

"Stand over there Miss so we can watch you."

I was appalled. I had never been treated that way before. I was dressed very nicely and was embarrassed. I wore a stylish neat dress and high heels. I looked like a Sunday school teacher! I worked for the telephone company! I lived at home with my parents!

Yet, there I stood in the middle of the sidewalk on the quiet Orange Circle Plaza Square. About twenty uniformed and plain clothes officers in suits faced me with revolvers drawn and shot guns aimed at me.

It was like a firing squad, and I was going to be publicly shot, as if Richard and I were "Bonnie and Clyde!"

"PUT YOUR HANDS ON YOUR HEAD," one officer ordered.

"Are you serious?" I asked politely. "What's going on?"

"JUST GET YOUR HANDS UP!" I was ordered again in a way I thought was very harsh and disrespectful. I hesitated, in shock. I stared at them blankly. A few raised their guns appearing as though they were ready to shoot if I didn't comply.

"GET THEM UP, NOW!!!" I was ordered and nervously, gradually raised them.

"ON YOUR HEAD!" They commanded. I felt like crying and was worried that my slip would show beneath my dress as I raised my arms. People were gathering in small crowds to watch at a distance.

I immediately regretted wearing my bright orange dress trimmed in white that day. I stood out like a sore thumb with all the drab buildings behind me. My appearance was all I could think of. I was so humiliated! Wearing orange in the middle of Orange!

All guns pointed at me. I knew they were loaded. What if one went off accidentally? Yet, I was more embarrassed than afraid. They were police officers, sworn to protect. They wouldn't hurt me, would they?

Concerned citizens were now cautiously approaching some of the officers to ask what was going on. I wanted to know that answer as well. Someone from the local news was filming the scene. If this was broadcast on television, I would be devastated!

"Am I getting a traffic citation?" I called out with a shaking voice. That's all I could think of as a possible reason, although I'd never seen a reaction like this for a traffic ticket.

No one replied. With guns heavily aimed at me, the officers just stared, somewhat perplexed. It became apparent I was naïve. They softened their attitude.

A rotund Orange police officer with a kind face approached the firing squad and talked to them. Whatever he told them made a few of them laugh. Soon, they all lowered their shot guns and returned their revolvers to their hidden holsters.

I got the impression some of them thought of themselves as Elliott Ness from an old movie. They now ignored me and walked away. So tense and attentive to me just seconds ago, I was now nothing to them. I remained standing still, waiting for orders.

"Can I put my hands down now?" I called out as they were leaving. No one answered or looked back. I stood still, afraid to move. With shaky arms, I began to lower them gradually. I dared not move, although they seemed to be abandoning me and no one aimed a gun.

Finally, the friendly rotund cop approached me and asked that I follow him in my car to the police station to answer a few questions. I asked if I was in trouble. I wasn't.

"Where's Richard, what's going on?"

"We got a call that he was wanted by the F.B.I." The friendly cop explained.

"The F.B.I.?" I was shocked. "What did he do?" Every possible heinous crime, including murder came to mind.

"He's a draft dodger." His reply was flat, but serious.

"Oh." I replied, relieved. Draft dodgers were everywhere.

After a while, Richard was released on the promise that he would report his current address to the draft board when they opened on Monday morning. Of course, he agreed.

Apparently the hotel clerk had called the police after jotting down my license plate number. It was reported that someone wanted by the F.B.I. was in my car. They didn't know it was because of the draft until they had him in custody.

Was that the way draft dodgers and their companions were treated? We never really knew the answer.

After reporting his address to Selective Service, Richard was told he would hear from them in a few weeks. During that time he was nervous about the draft.

"I can't go into the Army," he told me repeatedly.

"Are you afraid to go to Vietnam because you might get killed?"

"No, it's not that."

"Well then, it's only two years. That will go by quickly."

"No, I wouldn't last that long."

When I questioned him, he explained, "I would go crazy. I don't want to be owned by the government. I couldn't take orders and not be free to make my own choices. I'd rather be dead than go through that."

Because it was the philosophy of the times, his answer was not unusual.

When the dreaded letter from Selective Service arrived, Richard held it in his hand unopened. He stared at it with a sickly expression.

"Just open the darn thing!" I blurted out after a few moments. "It's going to say the same thing whether you open it or not."

Methodically, he began to open it, slowly peeling the paper and removing its contents. I watched him as he read the letter.

Suddenly, he threw it into the air, tossed his head back, closed his eyes, and smiled.

He never knew the reason why Selective Service made their determination. He was afraid to ask, just in case it was an error and they'd change their minds.

I picked the letter up from the floor.

"Go ahead, read it for yourself. Tell me what it says. I just want to hear it." Richard's voice was raspy, almost a whisper.

"You've been classified 4-F."

I don't think I ever saw Richard smile as widely as when I read the definition of that term: "Registrant is not qualified for any military service."

If anyone was ever happy about being rejected, it was Richard at that moment!

9. Cuckoo Clocks

Imagine palm trees swaying high above in the breeze, and below stars decorating the sidewalks honoring celebrities. Somewhere in between two overgrown kids walk hand in hand loudly singing famous "show tunes" and old classic hits late at night. They don't care if anyone hears them.

They are happy in the moment, and that's all that matters. Some of the craziest occasions in life can often be the most cherished.

He wears a seal-skin headband and she wears a suede leather jacket, fringed along the arms and waist, decorated with colorful beads. He sings in deep alto, and she in high soprano.

"Ooooooooooo-kla-homa,*" and "Oh sole mi-oooooo" were favorites, along with a duet of "Some enchanted evening; you will see a stranger."*

Their combined voices echo through the dark streets lit by occasional street lamps and the glares of passing headlights.

"Living for the moment" was the carefree hippie way, but the rent had to be paid.

*"Oklahoma" and "Some Enchanted Evening" are show tunes by Rodgers and Hammerstein.

Richard rented a bachelor apartment on Highland Avenue in Hollywood that cost $25 a week, and that's usually how he paid it, by the week.

It took that long to gather the money, and sometimes he was a few days late. When that happened he dreaded approaching the landlady. He would ask me to come along, hoping she would be friendlier. She wasn't.

She was like an angry principal and we were the bad kids in her office. Besides that, she was a little strange.

Her apartment always emitted damp steam that smelled like a cross between gym socks and boiling brussel sprouts. It was a foul unpleasant odor that seeped through the hallways, creeping under the doors of the apartments on the main floor. When nearing her apartment you felt like heaving. Richard was glad to be on the third floor.

He would pay the rent as she sat in a wheel chair on the other side of the half door. It was more like a throne, and she was as charming as a wicked witch in an old cartoon. I don't think she needed the chair because she would get out of it if necessary and walk without a problem.

Plastic containers of medicine were scattered everywhere, but her collection of clocks was most unusual. There were at least 200 of them of all designs, shapes and sizes. Covering the walls and tables, they left little room for anything else, except her medicine.

A few of the clocks were ornately styled brass, flowery and old fashioned. Some were made from carved wood. Several were plain and made of plastic, a few of those had cute animal faces or looked like cartoon characters.

58

Others were a mix of traditional and unusual, but the most interesting ones were a variety of cuckoo clocks, at least a half dozen or more on each wall.

Once, trying to be nice and hoping to get a smile from her grumpy frown, I complimented her assortment; but she just stared at me with a scowl.

I could understand clocks as collector's items, but she had all of them running at once; and the dozens of wind-up ones ticked very loudly, but of course, not in unison.

It sounded a little maddening with the loud *TICK-TOCK, TICK-TOCK, TICK-TOCK*, at different beats, coming from all areas of the room. There could be no peace in that place and I wondered how she could live that way.

We would sometimes see her devoted husband scurrying around the room, hurriedly checking that all the clocks were working, and setting the alarms on each one so they would ring/chime/beep/sing/chirp/or play music all at the same time. That seemed to be his whole purpose and duty in life while she collected the rent.

We were told by some of the other young tenants to pay the rent exactly on the hour to see what would happen.

Intrigued, we approached her half-door within a few minutes before one o'clock. Richard handed over the rent money just when the hour was about to strike. We waited in anticipation for what would happen next.

She was just signing the receipt when the hour struck. What a jubilee we witnessed!

Immediately on the hour, I was startled by numerous Cuckoo birds as they flung out of the dozens of clocks around the room. They were the first I noticed because of the thuds from little doors swinging open everywhere, and "CUCKOO, CUCKOO, CUCKOO repeated over and over at different intervals with a contrasting series of sounds.

Tiny German peasants emerged from one to dance around in and out of the clock to a lively polka. Alarms simultaneously rang from every corner, near the ceiling, near the floor, some loud and angry, some softly demanding attention.

Wind up clocks sitting on the tables rang so hard they vibrated in a mad sort of nervous dance. One shook so much it fell off the table. Westminster chimes with a variety of tones joined the insane reverberation of noises. None were synchronized.

It was loud and crazed madness. We stood amazed, watching and listening to the clocks as they came to life.

Most interesting was the landlady's reaction. She immediately stopped what she was doing; left the receipt unsigned, and sprung up from the wheel chair. A strange joy came over the woman. She was so euphoric, and so excited, she was overcome with excitement.

She turned to her husband who embraced her. Holding her in his arms, they danced to the madness while smiling and laughing, sharing their special happiness.

This was the glorious moment they had been waiting for – the joy of the clocks on the hour! The mixture of sounds invigorated her to sheer ecstasy. They were both so elated; they had tears in their eyes.

When the hour had struck and passed, it was over. She gradually contained herself. The smile and color drained from her face. She frowned as usual, adjusted her muu-muu dress, plopped heavily down into her chair, handed us the receipt, and closed her door, shutting us out with a slam.

Why they welcomed each hour was beyond our young comprehension.

Maybe they were like Richard, me, and the cuckoo clocks. Happy in the moment, we just cherished a seemingly crazy, but simple spark in time.

We just considered her weird, and thereafter Richard paid the rent and left as quickly as possible.

10. The Elevator Ride

One summer in the late sixties, there was a Sunday I will never forget. Richard rented a small apartment in a hilly area of Hollywood.

While gazing out the back kitchen window, he called me over to take a look. In the distance we could see an unusual tower nestled on a nearby hillside. The mystery of that tower called him to go exploring, and he would take me with him. We were young and adventurous.

While walking along the busy street, we discovered a foot path bordered by trees and wild brush hidden from the view of speeding traffic. We entered.

Soon the path became a paved sidewalk leading upward through a middle class neighborhood of older homes scattered along the way. Colorful flowering hedges and neat lawns greeted us at every turn. The sweet scent of honeysuckle blossoms permeated the soft breeze.

At first we enjoyed our walk and the sense of tranquility that surrounded us. Yet, it was unusually quiet and there wasn't a soul to be seen.

As the sun reached its highest point, we reached the top of the hill. We could see the tower now, but it was not accessible to us and not as mysterious up close. Annoying Richard, I complained several times that it was a long walk for nothing.

Our curiosity had been satisfied. Now, tired and thirsty, we just wanted to go home. The air was suddenly hot and we were exhausted from climbing the many stairs that led us there. We stopped to rest in the shade for a while before walking back down the long path to the busy avenue.

Nearby we noticed an unusual structure centered within wooden rails and a platform. It appeared to be primitively constructed of wood and metal and consisted of a dangling crate-like compartment that was suspended by a large cable.

We guessed it was an old outdoor elevator designed to be lowered to the bottom of the hilly community. It was probably built about the same time as many of the vintage houses, although we didn't know for sure.

Leaning on the rails surrounding the old elevator, we could see the landing far below. As we gazed at the long way down, we realized how far we had walked. We dreaded all those stairs in the afternoon heat. Suddenly a stranger appeared, seemingly out of nowhere.

Stranger than strange, he was a tall young man, thin, with a long nose, slightly long hair, and a shifty look in his eyes. Although he seemed to be just a friendly hippie, he gave me the creeps.

He commented about the hot sun and how tired we must be after walking all the way up there. As though he read our thoughts, he emphasized what a long walk it would be back down the hill.

"Why don't you just take the elevator down with me?" His smile seemed disarming, but there was something peculiar about him.

"Yeah, it would be better than walking all that way," Richard agreed.

"It sure would be a lot faster." The man nodded as he spoke.

Still suspicious, I protested: "That elevator is obviously old, and probably doesn't even work."

Grimacing with disgust at my apparent foolishness, the stranger mocked me.

"Look, I've lived here all my life, and I use this elevator every day. There isn't a thing wrong with it. If you walk down the hill, you're just acting stubborn and stupid.

Now angry, I grabbed Richard's arm to leave. "Well, we ARE walking down! Thanks anyway."

To my dismay, Richard pulled away and argued that he was tired and thirsty. If I wanted to walk down, I could just go alone.

"By the time you join us, we'll be at rest, peacefully beneath a tall oak tree." The stranger mused. It was an odd comment, but I didn't have time to give it much thought.

"Yeah, see you later!" Richard sneered. I think he was getting back at me for complaining so much. He left with the stranger.

After thinking it over for a second or two, I decided I didn't want to walk all that way alone. Rejecting my better judgment, I succumbed to the pressure of my companions.

Feeling defeated, I reluctantly dragged myself into the dangling structure. Once inside, it felt sturdy enough. The stranger kept assuring us that it was fine and there was absolutely nothing to worry about. He smirked at me in a way that made me want to hit him.

"It will soon be all over." He grinned mysteriously. I thought about that statement. It could be taken a few ways and I didn't like what I was thinking. What would soon be all over? Our lives? Our body parts? But there wasn't much time to think. The stranger released the lever.

The elevator slightly heaved, like an awakening monster. Suddenly it dropped with a jolt and remained still for a moment.

We all felt uneasy with anticipation as it dangled in midair. Frightened, I wanted out, but we had dropped about two or three feet. Just as I looked for an escape, the elevator jolted again. Then it began its long descent, slowly at first.

The resonance of metal scraping metal increased gradually. The ancient pulleys and suspension cables started to screech. Soon a chain broke loose and clanked against the top of the structure, scolding like an unheeded warning.

As the elevator increased its speed, the grinding became louder. It sounded like metal slowly ripping apart.

We dropped faster and faster as the screeching became louder and louder. The elevator began to howl like a fiend escaping Hell.

Down, down, down! The wooden crate that held our lives raced as though we were suspended by a loose rubber band stretching to its limit and ready to break. Piercing our ears, the screeching metal became so loud it echoed throughout the hills. It seemed to do the screaming for me because I couldn't. I was frozen and breathless.

I quickly glanced at the stranger for help or an explanation, or something, but was amazed that he appeared delighted.

He was actually smiling, excited with the madness of the wild ride. His eyes lit up as they met mine, as if we were about to share a grand moment together. I looked at him defiantly and thought: "Not even in your dreams, buddy."

My guardian angel and the devil had met to do battle during that moment locked in time. I wondered who would be the victor.

While my mind raced, I clung to the side of the elevator as it raced, plummeting downward, picking up speed like an amusement ride gone mad.

The speeding crate and screeching cable foretold death in my ears. I visualized the three of us like smashed pumpkins when we hit bottom.

Losing our balance, we were jostled about like rag dolls, tumbling on top of each other. Then the elevator struck the ground, tipped slightly, took its final breath, and settled with a loud flat thud. All was still and strangely silent. The ride was over.

Picking myself up, I checked to see if I was in one piece. We were greatly shaken, but intact. Richard's hand raced to grab the door handle, but so did mine.

"Let me! You almost got us killed!" Angry at Richard, I pulled his hand away and yanked the door open myself. Then we faced a somber crowd staring in silent shock.

The screeching cable had drawn attention from everyone in the area. How could it not? Neighbors gathered at the landing to witness the crash. They seemed worried, ready to help the injured, expecting tragic results.

They watched us emerge. There must have been something irritating in our youthful blank expressions that transformed their concerns into furious anger. They almost seemed disappointed we were alive and safe. Formerly kind and caring, they suddenly became a lynch mob within seconds!

"Call the police!" Someone shouted. "Those crazy kids were trespassing!" Someone else ran inside, most likely to call. Then more voices shouted.

Mostly middle aged folks with manicured lawns, they seemed to want to rip us apart with their bare hands – like crab grass from a perfect lawn.

"Were you looking for a joyride?" A woman in hair curlers and a house dress yelled. She flicked the ash off her cigarette when she finished her question.

"Crazy kids! What were you thinking? You're lucky to be alive! Can't you read? Didn't you see the *DANGER KEEP OUT* sign?" Voices shouted from different directions.

While I was contemplating how we would pay for any damages, Richard firmly grabbed my arm and hurried us away.

"Just keep walking. Don't look back." He whispered between clenched teeth.

"But won't we get in trouble?" I muttered, unable to think.

"Yeah, we will if we don't get out of here." With that warning, I picked up a quicker pace.

Finally, we could hear the busy traffic of the street below. We would soon be safe and home in minutes. We sighed with relief.

Regaining my composure, I began scolding Richard for getting on the elevator. He argued that I could have walked down, and no one forced me. I suddenly remembered the sign someone had mentioned.

"Hey, I didn't see a *DANGER KEEP OUT* sign, did you?" I asked Richard as he was looking back to make sure no one was following.

"No, but who cares?"

Suddenly the stranger emerged from the trees ahead of us, just like he did before. Startled, we stopped, not knowing what to expect. He was grinning.

"Just to let you know, there *was* a *DANGER KEEP OUT* sign, but I removed it."

We stood speechless, wondering how he was able to get ahead of us. Puzzled, we stared blankly.

"I hid the sign," he confessed.

I hoped Richard would slug him, but he just stood there motionless.

"I guess it just wasn't meant to be," the stranger continued.

Stunned, I glared at him. I must have had fire in my eyes. He smugly continued.

"We should all be dead right now, but we're not." He sighed. "Maybe it just wasn't meant for all of us to die.

With a crazed look, he gazed off in deep contemplation at the thought.

"Just what are you talking about?" I growled, fuming with impatience.

The stranger's eyes danced; he appeared unstable.

"I wanted to end my life. I knew that elevator was broken and decided that would be a good way to go. I hid the sign and waited for someone to come along. When I saw you two, I decided to take you with me."

"Why?" I demanded an answer. "Why did you want *us* to die with you?"

He shrugged his shoulders and explained.

"Well, I'll admit it, I'm a coward." He continued flatly, "I wanted to kill myself, but I didn't want to die alone."

We stood in silence for a moment.

Richard nudged my elbow to keep quiet. He nodded politely to the stranger and then rushed us both back to the safety of the busy street below.

I've had a lot of adventures in my life, but every time I ride an elevator, I think of that stranger.

11. Long Beautiful Hair

We passed the theater on Sunset Boulevard in Hollywood several times in the past few weeks. A famous and controversial play was to be shown there. Just about a half a block away, we noticed a young man hurrying on foot in its direction.

"What's up? What's going on?" Richard was curious about the man's urgency.

"Oh, we're getting the theater ready for a show tonight, and I'm a little nervous."

"Imagine how the guys running it must feel." Richard joked.

"I don't need to imagine, I'm one of them!"

"Do you need any help, I'm available to work." Richard was always open to opportunities that may come his way.

"No, sorry. We have all the people we need, but I can get you into the show for free. Would you two like to attend tonight's performance of *Hair*?" *

"What's that?" Richard asked.

"Richard, are you kidding? They've had it advertised on that sign for weeks. We'd love to go!" I quickly replied.

71

"Great, go to the ticket booth, give them my name and tell them I said to let you in free."

I memorized his name. I was so excited.

"I'm not going to some stupid play. I hate plays." Richard commented.

"We are going. You'll like it. Besides, it's a play about hippies." I had no idea if Richard would like it or not, but I knew I would, so we were going.

When we arrived, we were told to wait until everyone had been seated, and the show was just about to begin.

We were then allowed in and told to sit in any available seats. If someone showed up with tickets to those seats, we would have to give them up and find other seats, but that was O.K. with us.

The play was a musical and I enjoyed the songs; many became very popular, especially "The Age of Aquarius." *

The play captured the spirit of hippies and was very lively, but had a sad ending. I don't like sad endings.

One scene had nudity and the audience reacted with excited interest, everyone tried to get a closer look. There were loud whispers throughout the audience. Nudity in the theater was controversial. Our seats were a distance away and I didn't see anyone nude. Richard claimed he did, but added "it was stupid."

---

*__Hair: The American Tribal Love-Rock Musical__ was a controversial rock musical about hippies and draft dodgers. *"The Age of Aquarius" released by The 5th Dimension, 1969.

After the lights came on and the play was over, people stood and began to wander to the exits. I thought the theater would be filled with younger people, but from what I could see, most were older and some looked like grandparents. Within the crowd nearest to us, we were the youngest couple.

Some people began to point to us. "Over there, let's get their autographs!" At once, they began to surround us with admiring worship. "You kids were just great!"

"We loved your play!"

People were pushing their way toward us holding out their programs and pens begging for our autographs.

"I wasn't in the play." I admitted.

"Oh, honey, yes you were." The older lady with white curls and a bright red lipstick smile insisted, shoving her program at me.

I turned to see Richard actually signing his autograph. The lady I refused was now getting in line with others to ask Richard.

"Richard!" I scolded him and then announced to the others: "He wasn't in the play either!"

"That's O.K. we love you anyway." They began to pat us on the back or affectionately take our hand or arm.

One lady gently touched the suede of my fringed leather jacket. When she noticed one of the little beads, she asked about them.

The people were fascinated with us. We were heroes to them. They had been uplifted by the hippie ideology presented in the play.

The music stirred up emotions of love, joy, youth, and freedom of expression -- everything wonderful in this world. It's amazing what a good play can do to for a person's spirit. They seemed to be flying high on the concept of peace, love and brotherhood as it was presented to them.

How magnificent it seemed at the moment for us to have so much attention and admiration!

By the time we exited, Richard and I were slightly euphoric from all the affection bestowed upon us. It was a great feeling, but oddly surreal.

When we walked a short distance from the theater and away from its lights and our fans, it grew quieter and darker. Alone, we were "nobodies" again.

That was normal for us, but I thought how sad it must be for "fallen stars." Such fame and admiration cannot last forever; not even for a couple of charlatans.

12. Bel Aire Baloney

One day Richard was hired to work at a multi-million dollar home in the exclusive Bel Aire area of Hollywood. The wealthy couple wanted him to place ice plants along their steep hillside. He was hoping to earn $20.00 for a day's work, but ended up with $40.00 for two hours work and a trip to the emergency room.

Ice plants are popular on hillsides in California for their succulent green spears and flowers that create a dense carpet. The difficulty is planting them. A person needs to crawl up the steep hillside to place the ice plants into the ground.

Now Richard never was one who enjoyed working outside in the hot sun, especially on a steep hillside, but he needed the money and was willing to give it a try.

With his big combat boots slipping in the loose soil and his feet hot within the leather, he lost his footing and slid on his belly all the way down the steep hill and right smack into the back yard of the wealthy couple who hired him.

Smudged with soil, he was still clutching an ice plant in one hand and a small trowel in the other. His left leg was somewhat twisted and bent beneath him.

The multi-millionaire helped Richard to his feet, dirty and smelly as he was. Limping and moaning, Richard leaned on him as he hobbled along. The rich man helped him into his brand new pristine Bentley with its white leather interior.

When Richard got out, there was soil all over the seat and floor. He felt badly about it, but was surprised when the billionaire didn't seem to mind.

Richard had been treated with genuine concern, consideration and kindness to which he was not accustomed, but immensely enjoyed.

When I saw him, his leg was wrapped in bandages; he was limping on crutches, and moaning in agony. He reached out for me as I helped him make it to the couch to sit down and rest.

'"Oh, the pain! Oh, the pain!" He moaned and groaned.

"What happened?"

"I fell down the hill. They took me to the emergency room."

Seeing my look of panic, he assured me: "It was all covered by their insurance company, so don't worry."

"Oh, you poor thing!" I brought a glass of lemonade and pillows to comfort him. I pampered and fussed over him.

Then he did something only Richard would do. He stood up on both legs. I was shocked.

"No, you'll hurt yourself. You'll make it worse!"

76

He grinned, and then threw the crutches aside. My jaw dropped as I watched.

"What are you doing, are you crazy?" With theatrical exaggeration, Richard lifted his injured foot onto the coffee table, knee upright, and then began to remove the wrappings from his leg, leaning on it as he did so. I was bewildered at this point.

"What did they give you for pain? Are you on some heavy medication?" I asked.

He just smiled and when his leg was completely unwrapped, he jumped up and danced on it, round and round.

He grabbed my arm and swung me in circles, dancing happily. Then he did his rendition of an Irish jig and a tap dance.

"Stop, stop, you'll hurt yourself!" I pulled his arm, trying to make him sit down.

When he was finally worn out, he caught his breath, laughed, and sat down.

"Explain!" I frowned at him. He just grinned.

"Don't get mad at me; I'll tell you what happened."

"This better be good." I yanked one of the pillows away from him and used it for myself instead.

"Alright, I climbed the hill and planted about a hundred of those stupid ice plants, and then I just couldn't take it anymore. It was so hot. The sun was beating down. That hill was so steep, I couldn't sit or stand. I had to kind of lay on my stomach and crawl, dragging those plants. It was too much."

"And so, Richard, what happened?" I was expecting to hear some goofy story, and I did.

"I just wanted to quit. I didn't know how to tell them. They were so nice."

"O.K, I can see where this is going."

He paused, taking another long drink of lemonade, clinking the ice to make it colder, and then smacked his lips.

"Aaaah." He sat back and put both arms under his head.

"And then…" I was growing impatient.

"And then," he continued, "I wanted to get away from those plants, so I just let myself go. As I slid, half the ones I planted uprooted and toppled down the hill with me. It was pretty bad."

"So you slid down the hill on purpose?"

"Well yeah, sort of, I guess. It wasn't preplanned. It just happened."

"OK, then what?"

"Well, as I hit bottom I kind of twisted my ankle. It really did hurt at first.

I stared at him, listening closely.

"They were being so nice to me. I kind of liked the special treatment. After they went through all the trouble to take me to the emergency room, I had to exaggerate to the doctor." He argued in self-defense.

"Oh, Richard, that's terrible. You should have just told them it was too hot."

"I couldn't do that. It was too late. So here I am."

"Here you are," I flatly echoed.

"Here I am," he repeated.

"Richard, you are so full of baloney. You faked an injury."

"They thought I was hurt, what was I supposed to do?"

I told him what I thought he should do.

The next day, Richard called the couple. "I'm feeling better, but I don't think I will be able to finish the planting job. You might want to get someone else to do it."

"Of course, of course we will. We understand. Please stop by, we would like to pay you for your work. We feel so badly about your injury."

After hearing that, Richard told them he would be over tomorrow afternoon. The time was set and off he went, taking me along with him.

"Wow, I only worked two hours, uprooted the ones I planted, and got his Bentley dirty; I didn't think they'd pay me a penny!"

We arrived at the multi-million dollar mansion in one of the most exclusive areas of Hollywood. We came in through the back kitchen door, but didn't think twice. I suppose I expected the home to be something out of the ordinary, but basically it was just a house with a kitchen, dining room, living room, like any other house, but very large and nice of course.

The couple welcomed us. As we sat at their dining room table drinking ice tea, the man stared at me thoughtfully. He then commented about how much I looked like a starlet that was about my age. She was a popular young actress and I felt complimented.

Although others told me the same thing, I was particularly flattered because he knew her personally.

"I've been told I look like her before."

"I'm her dentist and you have the same teeth, mouth, and jaw structure." Leave it to a dentist to notice.

Richard sat beside me, his crutches leaning in the corner.

"The police really patrol this area. When I came here to work, they questioned me. I think they thought I was a burglar or something."

"Well, you know this is an exclusive neighborhood. They must protect people here, there are many celebrities." The dentist then motioned toward their large living room window.

"Look out the window. See that house over there?" He pointed, and we all looked.

"A famous suspense writer lives there. His stories have been made into movies. He had a television show. Can you guess who he is?"

I knew exactly who he was. I loved his stories.

"We often see him out there doing yard work. He seems to really enjoy it. Most people around here hire gardeners to take care of their lawns, but not him."

The wealthy dentist shook his head and chuckled. "What a sight to see, such a famous man with a garden hose in his hand, doing lawn work, like a common gardener."

"No kidding? That's hilarious!" Richard found that interesting. "You should ask *him* to place those ice plants on your hill."

Everyone laughed, but I kicked Richard's ankle under the table.

"No, of course I wouldn't do that." He replied with warmth and affection.

"There's nothing wrong with doing something you enjoy, and he likes to do his own yard work. Just because he can well afford to pay someone, why should he? He enjoys it and would rather do it himself. I admire him."

The dentist began to chuckle as he continued, "It's just kind of funny that you'd think he was the gardener instead of a celebrity if you saw him out there."

I thought of my dad who enjoyed working in the yard. I don't think wealth would stop him either.

As we talked about the neighborhood, the lady handed Richard an envelope. He opened it. They had paid him for a full day's work and included an extra twenty dollars.

Richard was ecstatic. "Wow, you didn't have to give me anything extra, that's really nice of you."

"Well, we wanted to give you a little something for your pain and suffering. Do you think that's enough?"

"Heck yeah," was Richard's reply.

The couple seemed pleased that he was content.

Richard wasn't really hurt as bad as he acted, so he actually felt a little guilty for taking the extra money, especially after my lecture the day before.

The wealthy dentist asked Richard to sign a few papers for "insurance purposes" to cover the doctor expenses and "legalities."

Richard began signing them without a second thought and stated something like "satisfied with compensation" and "will not hold responsible" or something like that.

After signing, the dentist carefully took the papers as though they were important documents. Both he and his wife seemed relieved and happy that task had been completed. Then his wife quickly changed the subject.

"Do you collect Blue Chip stamps?" The wealthy lady asked me.

"Sure, I do."

"Well I have a lot of them in my kitchen drawer. I'm sure there's enough to fill several booklets. Would you like to have them?"

"Sure, I don't even have a half a book." I commented. "Don't you want to redeem them?"

"No, I just save them." She admitted as she walked into the kitchen and opened a drawer.

I was surprised someone took the trouble of saving the stamps, but didn't redeem them.

Blue Chip Stamps were like Green Stamps and were given to customers according to the amount of money they spent at the store.

Smaller than the average postage stamp, you would fill pages in paper booklets. When filled, they could be redeemed for items in a catalog or at a redemption center. The higher the value of an item required a greater number of booklets.

She placed the stamps into a bag.

"My maid would like to have them, but I'll give them to you instead. " She smiled. "She's going to be so disappointed to find them gone." She seemed complacent with that thought.

I had a tiny tinge of sympathy for the maid, but I gladly took them from her hand.

"Why do you save them if you don't redeem them?"

"I really don't know." She seemed puzzled with the thought. "I guess I just can't bear to throw them away because they are worth something to someone, just not to me."

I didn't say anything in reply, but I was thinking she was like the writer who lived across the street. Both were wealthy, but enjoyed the simple satisfactions of the poor.

I once heard a famous comedian say his fondest memory was when he lived in a tiny apartment during winter. He wanted to turn the oven on to help keep warm, but would bake a potato for an excuse. Nothing was cozier than the warm kitchen and a simple baked potato. You'd think his fondest memory would be moving into a mansion, but it wasn't.

My mom once told me that poor people always have something the rich want, but can't buy with money. I never could figure that out. I thought it was the other way around.

Take Richard, for example, he loved to imagine himself wealthy. He had the ability to close his eyes and transcend to another reality.

A baloney sandwich on white bread with mustard and an orange could be a gourmet chef's specialty in his imagination. No matter what the meal, he always appreciated it.

"How can you eat that as if it was a gourmet meal prepared by a chef?" I asked.

He turned to me and grinned. "It's simple. I imagine I'm eating at the Ritz."

"The Ritz? What's that?

"It's a very expensive make believe restaurant. I imagine I'm rich, and I'm eating there. It's a wonderful place."

He told me whenever he was stuck someplace with no alternative, he would use his imagination to be somewhere else. It was his way of escaping when there was no real escape possible.

He visited exotic islands, mountain tops, and every tourist resort available to mankind. Richard had been to them all and had sampled all the wonderful foods that each place had to offer, all in his imagination!

When I would play along, I'd place his fried baloney on toast, cut in fancy wedges, onto a silver platter from a discount store. He made me feel like I was serving a prince.

He would graciously thank me. I loved that about him. He never complained about anything I served him and was always appreciative when I brought him food.

After leaving Bel Aire, we went straight to the Blue Chip Stamp Redemption Center in Los Angeles. I wanted something for Richard's little apartment.

While examining cookware, I noticed Richard strumming a folk guitar.

"Richard, you can't play the guitar!"

"Yeah, but maybe I can learn and play it when people visit. It would be really cool to have one, even if it just sat in the corner.

"Oh, what an ego trip!" I teased him.

Regardless, the stamps were traded for the guitar. When people came over, he would strum it. One visitor tried to teach him to play, but Richard became frustrated with it.

Eventually the guitar became nothing more than an ego trip sitting in the corner to impress others.

No matter if you're rich or poor, how much in life is just an ego trip? It could be a mansion in Bel Aire with a gardener, or a guitar in the corner of a hippie's apartment.

Although Richard ended up selling the guitar to pay his rent, he still enjoyed baloney sandwiches at the Ritz.

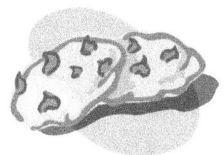

13. The Cookie Guy

One afternoon Richard and I were walking on Sunset Boulevard and wandered into one of the shops along the way that catered to tourists and the wealthy.

Richard immediately was drawn to the aroma of chocolate chip cookies spread upon a white paper doily

The sales girl was friendly. She noticed him as he admired the cookies. "Go ahead, take one. Those are free samples."

Richard was always hungry and never missed a chance for a free snack. He delicately placed one into his mouth and let it melt and savor there. His expression reflected an ascent to a heavenly plane.

"I love the walnuts," Richard's words were muffled as he munched. "May I have another?"

She smiled and replied, "Sure, go ahead." We're getting more today. We are expecting a delivery at any moment.

"Would you like to buy some?" she asked him.

"Umm, yeah, I'll think about that." His large paw reached for the last one; she didn't mind. I watched him stuff it into his mouth.

"We sell them by the bag," she gestured toward two small neat brown lunch sacks filled with cookies displayed on the counter. An older well-dressed lady approached and grabbed the two bags.

"They are the best chocolate chip cookies you could ever buy." Smiling she paid for the treasures and left the store. Richard's eyes followed the bags of cookies as they were taken out the door.

The salesgirl watched the lady exit. When the store was empty, she spoke in a low voice taking us into her confidence.

They're made by a guy in his apartment kitchen, using a family recipe!" She hesitated, and glanced toward the store window that faced the street. "See that guy with the cookies, that's him."

We watched the man emerge from an older V.W. bug. He was slender, and wore a round knit hat with bright bold colors in an African design. Although a little older, he was hip and casual, like us.

When entering the store, he carefully carried more of the brown paper lunch bags filled with cookies. He had a nice smile and was polite as he placed them gently on the counter.

We left the little shop on Sunset.

"What a great way to make money." I told Richard, You should do that." He was licking crumbs from his fingers and just grunted.

Years later, I discovered hundreds of packages made to appear like paper lunch bags filled with factory made chocolate chip cookies on all the store shelves. There were many similarities. The bag even had a picture of the guy who originally made them. He looked remarkably familiar.

If that was the same guy with the cookies from years ago, he must have worked hard and put lots of effort into making and selling those cookies. He became rich and famous!

On the other hand, Richard didn't.

14. The Celebrities

Have you ever wondered what it would be like to ride in the back of a Rolls Royce limousine driven by a chauffeur in Hollywood?

Richard and I were out walking on Sunset Boulevard toward the Strip one busy Saturday afternoon. As a couple we blended with other young people. None of the weekend tourists particularly noticed us. That changed within seconds, but only lasted minutes.

That day, we were instantly transformed into celebrities and the manner in which the world viewed us was impressive.

Living in Hollywood among celebrities, the movie industry, and the super wealthy, generated a sense of identity with them all, strange as it may seem.

When the sun shined and when it rained, it did so on the famous and on the unknown equally. Earthquakes jolted all of us. The streets on which the expensive cars rolled along were the same streets the cheap ones traveled. Even the air we breathed was the same shared by rich and poor alike.

Overlooking Hollywood is the famous landmark, the "H-O-L-L-Y-W-O-O-D" sign. It consists of huge white letters standing on a high hill above Hollywood. Tourists are fascinated with the sign.

Richard brought me up to Mulholland Drive to retrieve a shoe box full of treasures he once hid behind one of the letters for safe keeping.

Up close, the letters were just huge placards propped up on the hillside. Litter and debris had become trapped in the plant growth that surrounded them. At that time they needed painting and were a little battered.

From a close view, they appeared to be just an advertising billboard, a gimmick. How different they appeared up close compared to looking up at them from far below. They seemed huge, glamorous, and bigger than life, but when seeing them from a closer perspective, all their grandeur was lost. I thought the sign was like the movies Hollywood produced, illusions to the audience.

Often when we strolled along Hollywood Boulevard, we were offered free tickets to see some show that was being televised. They wanted to fill the studio with an audience and most anyone would do.

They flashed "applause" signs and expected you to enthusiastically participate. A few people near microphones stood close to the stage; they would clap, whistle, holler, and make other sounds to give the illusion the audience was excited. Although we were able to see a lot of famous people up close, we began to lose interest.

It was always the same, everything looked so big and glamorous on television, but in person everything was different. The stage was smaller, the celebrities were shorter and often not as attractive, or as entertaining.

We'd place our hands and feet in those of the stars, in the cement outside Grauman's Chinese Theater. It was fun at first, but it became more fun to watch the tourists. We even attended opening nights outside the theater, but even that grew stale with the crowds and stars who seemed superficial at times.

Richard slid down the steep hill to recover his shoe box of treasures. He swept away dirt, shrubbery and debris and removed his precious treasure from its hiding place. He then brought the box up to Mulholland to show me its contents.

Inside, were trinkets he saved, but the most treasured of all was a handful of poker chips. To me, they were no different than any other poker chips I had seen, but to Richard they meant so much more.

"These are souvenirs I took from a movie set when I was hired as an extra." Although Richard would embellish at times, he was serious about this.

"You were in a movie?" I was surprised. "How did that happen?"

"One day a movie studio sent a bus down Sunset picking up hippie guys with long hair and mustaches. They needed a lot of extras for a musical Western. The hippie guys already looked like they belonged in the old West."

"It probably saved time and money." I was thinking in a practical way.

"Yep, they picked me up with a whole bunch of guys that were just hanging out at Sunset and Vine."

"What did you do in the movie?"

"They gave us old time clothes and hats to wear and we sat at round tables, drinking, smoking, and playing cards with these poker chips."

"Well, that sounds easy and fun."

"Well, it wasn't. It was boring. All we did was wait, wait, wait, and wait some more."

"For what?"

"For scenes to be filmed. During all that waiting, we played cards. Everyone at our table became impatient, and then a couple of guys began arguing over the game. Well, one thing led to another and all five of us were thrown out. They told us to pick up our checks and leave the studio."

"What an opportunity you had for a great job, and lost!" I lamented.

"Being in a movie is not what you think it is. People always think it's so glamorous, but it's not. I would hate doing that all the time. All that waiting would make me crazy."

"I don't know, it sounds easy. Did they film any scenes with you in them?"

"Just the saloon scenes. When the movie comes out, look for me playing poker with these chips."

I watched him hold them fondly, as though they were golden. I suspected he was sorry for not being more patient, but proud to have been in a movie.

94

I took the poker chips from him and placed them carefully into the shoe box. I took him by the hand and led him away.

"Well today is a new day, let's see what it will bring."

We ended up on Sunset Boulevard. A friendly guy driving a Rolls Royce limousine called to us as we were crossing the street.

"Hey, you two want a ride down to Rodeo Drive in a Rolls Royce?"

"Are you serious, bro?" Richard's eyes lit up. That Rolls was so shiny you could see your reflection in the glossy paint.

It was early in the afternoon and tourist time. Richard pulled me by the hand and before I knew it we were both sitting in the back seat of the luxurious, gorgeous Rolls Royce limousine. The inside was beautiful and roomy beyond belief. The car was fabulous.

The driver was jovial and fun. As soon as we settled in, he placed a chauffeur's hat on his head.

"You guys are going to love this!" He smiled, nodding to us from the right side of the front seat.

"That's weird; he's driving from the passenger's side." I naively observed.

"That's because the car is from England." Richard responded knowingly.

The light changed and the driver shifted into gear. Richard complimented him on his beautiful car and asked why he invited us along.

"I just like to give ordinary people a ride in a Rolls limo so they know what it's like. Everyone should experience such luxury."

He continued, in a sort of solemn way: "Honestly, I have more fun taking people for rides in it than I do just driving it around by myself."

We lowered the windows and looked out at the tourists. They were staring at Richard and me as though we were wealthy and famous.

The driver laughed, "They think you two are movie stars! Look at them! They think you're somebody important just because you're riding in the back seat of a Rolls Royce!"

"Yeah, and they think you're our chauffeur." Richard waved and nodded to the excited tourists in a car that was driving alongside the limo in the next lane.

"Go ahead, wave to them." The driver told me as he glanced from the front seat. "See how it feels to be rich and famous."

I waved and smiled and the tourists in the crowded car began talking to each other in an excited way. I think they were brainstorming names of famous people we may have looked like and who we might have been. One was trying to take our picture. They looked ecstatic.

The driver was gawking and swaying his car a little as he looked at us. They were so happy to see a movie star; at least Richard had been in a movie.

As traffic moved on, more cars approached with the same reaction. I didn't know how to act, sometimes I'd smile and wave and other times I acted snobbish. It was funny, but kind of strange.

After a little while, I began to feel uncomfortable and I stopped looking out the window. Having people stare at me became annoying.

"Now you know what it's like to be wealthy!" Our driver laughed.

"You must be rich to own a car like this; what do you do for a living?" Richard was curious.

I'm a writer, but no different than anybody else. You know what makes me different? This car. That's all, and it's just a metal object. Doesn't mean a thing, without it, we're basically just people, not much different."

Richard liked the comparison and smiled while waving to another car full of admirers.

The writer continued: "No difference between you two and two celebrities."

"Except fame and money." I added.

"Yeah, so what? It means nothing." He seemed sad at first, but continued cheerfully. "It's all an illusion, nothing more."

He glanced back at us, "So, how does it feel to ride in a Rolls limo? Are you enjoying it?"

Richard commented, "Yeah, it's kind of nice to feel rich and important."

"How about you?" The writer asked me.

I was hesitant to answer. I had mixed feelings. He was anxious for a reply, but mine was delayed.

When we reached Rodeo Drive, the writer got out to open the door for us, just like a chauffeur.

"Here you are folks, at Rodeo Drive. Enjoy shopping!" It was obvious he loved play acting.

Neither one of us had any interest in shopping on Rodeo, even if we actually had lots of money to throw away.

As I exited, the writer held the door open and once again asked me how it felt to ride in a Rolls limo down Sunset Boulevard. I stood facing him, ready with an answer.

"Are you familiar with Emily Dickinson's poems?" I asked.

"I'm a writer, of course I am!"

"Then you'll know what I mean when I say I felt like a 'frog in a bog.'" *

He gazed at me with a momentary look of surprise, laughed heartily, and then drove on.

We later saw him offering a ride to another young hippie couple.

*Reference to Emily Dickinson's poem "I'm Nobody! Who are you?"

15. A Case of Mistaken Identity

Richard rented a small bachelor's apartment on Beachwood Drive in Hollywood. It was very close to an old movie studio owned by Columbia Pictures. We passed it whenever we were out walking.

It made me think about life itself with all its drama, and how people can be like actors just playing a part. Some moments in life are like scenes from a movie filled with action, adventure, surprise and drama.

We had a day like that in early 1969.

Hollywood during the sixties was exciting. Adding to that, it was populated by an array of characters. Hippies were harmless tourist attractions, somehow blending nicely with the others.

The criminal class was another element of society. Richard and I were not criminals; in fact we strived to stay out of trouble and away from those who found themselves in it.

One day we had an encounter with two men and learned something about judging people on face value.

Richard's apartment complex had a courtyard with

the entrance from Beachwood Drive. Each apartment had a door that overlooked the courtyard. They were like small connected cottages.

The windows in back faced a large private back yard. During spring, tall grass sweetly scented the fresh breeze that came through those windows. It was a peaceful, quiet place to live.

Whenever we went for a walk, I'd pick flowers along the way and place them in little jars and containers throughout the tiny apartment.

Richard originally rented apartment number nine. The Beatles had a song about "number nine" as a kind of symbol of "the end." *

Richard didn't like that and when apartment #13 became available the next month, he asked for it. Apparently, he didn't mind the superstition that "13" was unlucky. Adjacent to the laundry room, it would be quieter without having a neighbor on both sides.

Richard never met the previous tenant and knew nothing about him, just that he left abruptly and owed the landlady money. She was upset about it.

One day the Beatles were playing from Richard's beloved stereo: "Blackbird singing in the dead of night." **

I had just made lunch, and we were relaxing when there was a loud pounding on the front door. Richard seldom had visitors and didn't know anyone who would knock in such an assertive manner. He carefully peeked out the window.

*"Revolution Number 9" is from The Beatles *White Album*, 1968.
**"Blackbird" is from The Beatles *White Album*, 1968, Apple Records.

Quickly turning to me, his face looked like he'd seen a ghost. Approaching me closely, he whispered: "There are two plain clothes cops at the door."

I was puzzled. "Why?"

"I don't know." He stared at me blankly, and then panicked.

Racing around frantically trying to find a shirt to make himself presentable, he ransacked the closet, dropping hangers and tipping over a basket of clean laundry.

"Bam, Bam, Bam!" The pounding grew more insistent, demanding, intimidating.

I looked through a tiny opening in the slats of the blinds to see two men standing rigidly.

Dressed in dark suits, with white shirts and neckties, they were clean shaven, had neat haircuts, and wore conservative looking sun glasses and watches.

Richard told me plain clothes cops always wore watches.

They appeared anxious, and I nearly jumped as they impatiently struck the door again. This time the pounding sounded angry.

Now, I panicked and hurried to find a brush for my hair and straighten my own appearance.

The heavy thumping continued and shook the old wooden door.

"Should we open it?" We were ready, but hesitated.

"If we don't, they may break the door down."

"Or they'll ask the landlady for the key, and that would make her mad."

"O.K. You open the door and see what they want, and I'll go in the kitchen. It would be better if you talked to them first."

Richard knew I had a way of calming a situation. I would be cordial, and then he would casually appear from the kitchen doorway. It was only about twenty feet from the front door.

"O.K. you can open it." Richard whispered while poking his head out from the kitchen. "Act casual and be nice to them."

After one last glance into the mirror to freshen my lipstick, I slowly opened the deadbolt lock on the door.

The unlatching of the top lock was loud enough for the men to hear. The knocking stopped. All was silent. I could almost feel the tension on the other side of the door

While I strived to be calm and friendly, I slowly turned the doorknob. I intended to just open it a few inches, very slightly, just to show my cooperative smile.

The two men stood, one behind the other. The first one grabbed the edge of the door, shoving it so hard it struck my arm and knocked me to the floor.

Within a split second I was overpowered and both men stood inside the apartment. I was surprised and helpless.

The second man kept his hand firmly on the door handle, closing it enough to keep me from running out and from others looking in, but open enough for a quick escape. Both seemed nervous and jumpy.

The man in front stood closest to me. My eyes were drawn to a yellow sweater that was draped over his hand. I could see the black barrel of an automatic handgun partially concealed beneath it.

He held the gun tightly while his finger gripped the trigger. Wide-eyed, with his hand slightly trembling, he nervously waved the gun in all directions. As he scanned the tiny apartment, he seemed ready to shoot at anything.

"Who is it?" Richard sounded friendly as he emerged from the kitchen, casually drying his hands.

The gunman aimed directly at him with a steady hand. I thought he would fire it.

I gasped and froze.

Suddenly the other guy blurted: "No, don't take him. He's not the guy. It's not him!"

His voice sounded frantic, but Richard did not hear him. Instead, he noticed me sitting on the floor near the front door. He looked puzzled.

"What happened?"

"I fell when they came in."

The two men suddenly became very friendly. "Oh, we're sorry miss, are you O.K.?"

As one of them attempted to help me up, I noticed the other one sigh with relief, and then craftily slip the handgun into his side pocket. He rolled up the yellow sweater and hastily tucked it under his arm.

Apparently, they weren't aware that I had seen the gun. I hurried to stand on my own without their help and remained quiet.

Overly friendly, the men asked if they could sit down for a moment.

"Of course, make yourself at home." Richard was glad to oblige the officers.

"We're sorry for disturbing you; we thought you were somebody else. Is there another guy named Freddie, who lives here, too?

"No, just me."

"Did you move in recently?"

"Yeah, just a few weeks ago."

"Oh, then Freddie must have moved out." He faced his friend who nodded.

"Do you think he'll be coming around here again?"

"No, he owes the landlady money, and she's a tough old bird. Why don't you ask her about him?"

He smiled, and then turned to me.

"We're really sorry about all this. I hope you guys are OK with us, and accept our apology."

Richard grinned happily: "Of course."

"I mean, we wouldn't have busted through the door like that, but you took so long to open it. We thought you were stalling or hiding from us. We didn't know what was going on. You got us a little worried there."

"Oh, that's O.K. no harm done."

"So you're cool with us?"

"Yeah, yeah. We're cool." Richard wasn't accustomed to police apologies, but I could tell he kind of liked it.

"So, uh, when we walk out of here, you guys aren't going to call the cops and report us or anything?" The man was carefully testing the waters, so to speak.

"Call the cops?" Richard was shocked. "You mean you two aren't cops?"

The two men looked at each other and began laughing.

"Us cops? You thought we were cops? That's funny!" They seemed entertained by the idea. After chuckling for a few minutes they became serious.

"We don't like cops. No wonder you didn't open the door. Nobody likes cops coming around. So, I believe you when you tell us you won't be calling them on us."

"No, I don't like cops either, we won't call them; we're cool."

"Thanks. You're good people." They stood, ready to leave.

"Imagine that! We thought you were Freddie, and you thought we were the cops!" They laughed again.

"Just a case of mistaken identity!"

As they stood, I could see the outline of the handgun in the man's side pocket.

They said good-bye and told us to have a nice day.

I watched them step into the courtyard, casually at first, then pick up their pace and hurry away.

Relieved, Richard sat down.

"Wow, I really thought those two were cops."

I looked at him, finally able to speak. "It would have been better if they were cops."

"Why the heck would you say that?" Richard looked confused.

"One of them had a handgun with his finger on the trigger. It was aimed at you, until the other guy told him not to shoot. You could be dead right now!

Richard looked sick.

"Yeah, and you would be a dead witness."

Turning the stereo on, Richard hoped it would help us to relax. The Beatles were singing "Happiness is a Warm Gun." *

Immediately switching it off, Richard turned the television on instead.

*"Happiness is a Warm Gun" is from The Beatles *White Album*, 1968, Apple Records.

16. Going up the Country

We were "going up the country,"* traveling along Pacific Coast Highway on a quest to find a commune. Someone said there was one nestled in the hills of Big Sur, along the coast near Monterey, California.

I wanted to experience a commune where people lived in harmony and believed in peace, love and brotherhood. I was an idealist.

Richard on the other hand, was a realist. He didn't buy into the flowery ideals. People just weren't that good.

That was his opinion, not mine; but like my dad often told me "you have a lot to learn."

As we drove along Coast highway, majestic scenery greeted us with pristine ocean views and steep cliffs.

Richard thought it was the most beautiful place in the world. He felt a sense of peace there. He told me about a time when he hitchhiked through the area. Alone with nowhere to stay, he laid out his sleeping bag and slept on the beach.

*"Going up the Country," by Canned Heat, 1968 Liberty Label.

The next morning he awoke to find he was not alone. Tiny sand crabs had crawled into the sleeping bag with him. He freaked out, jumped up, shook out the sleeping bag and watched as they scurried away. Although, he said he'd rather have those nestled in his sleeping bag than a snake, like on a previous occasion.

The highway was sometimes winding and dangerous with rocks on one side leading up steep mountain sides, and sudden ledges leading down to the waves crashing along the shore. Beautiful and breathtaking, driving was a little frightening at times.

We decided to pull off the highway and drove up a dirt road to explore. We parked "Old Blue"(my car) in a farmer's field on a hill near a fenced-in cow.

After admiring the beauty of nature, it soon became cold and we were shrouded in a damp thick mist. It then began to rain. We found refuge inside the car and waited for the rain to stop.

When the weather cleared, we tried to start Blue. It sputtered on the damp foggy hillside. After flooding it with gas because of too much pedal pumping, we had to let it sit for a while. We tried to push it, but Blue was stuck in the mud created by the rain.

Unfortunately, the farmer who owned the land drove past and discovered us.

"Hey, what do you think you're doing on my land?"

"We just liked it here and thought we'd enjoy the scenery."

"What are you, a couple of gypsies?"

"No, we were just passing through."

"And of all the land around here to park your car on, you chose mine?"

We didn't give an answer or an excuse. We had none to give.

"Well, never mind. Just get your car off my property. I want it gone, along with the two of you, by the time I come back this way. If it's not, I'll call the Sheriff and have you charged for trespassing."

Richard was apologetic. "We're sorry, sir. We'll leave right away."

We didn't want to tell him we were stuck in the mud on his private property. He was already mad at us. He drove off grumpily.

Not wanting to get into trouble, we walked down the hill hoping to get help from someone who could give us a push.

We found a long haired guy wearing a head band and a green army jacket. From his appearance, we assumed he would be someone we could trust and would help us. It was better than asking the grumpy farmer

He was driving a sturdy Jeep with bells dangling from the rear view mirror. Although he did pull over when we waved at him, he didn't talk much.

He had an intense "far off" stare and I wondered what he was thinking. He agreed to drive us back up the hill and give Blue a push off the land and onto the road.

We explained that once we got the car on the road, we could "pop start" it by letting it roll down the hill. That was the plan, anyway.

Each time the driver hit a bump the bells on the mirror jingled. I thought they were pretty cool at first, but they soon became irritating. His jeep only had a front seat.

I sat between Richard and the driver; he was kind of strange. We showed him where the car was located and he gave Blue a push, and then a shove, and then a fully forced *slam!* The old car didn't budge.

Frustrated, he soon became obsessed with forcing it to move, but it wouldn't, not even an inch! He began to plow into it. Again, it remained solidly in the mud.

Richard and I got out of his Jeep and out of the way before he ran us over. We were helpless to stop him. He was all over the hill, approaching the car at every angle, his Jeep's engine was smoking and overheated. He didn't seem to care.

He attacked the sides, first on one side and then the other, denting the strong steel in several places. He just kept ramming it over and over again. All the while, he kept his blank stare just as he did before. *"Bang, slam, bam, clunk!"*

When we tried to call to him, begging him to stop, he didn't seem to hear. He struck the old Ford so hard from behind, that it tipped upward and stood on its bumper with the other end standing straight into the air, balancing precariously.

We had never seen a car standing straight up. That's when the farmer returned. He had another guy with him. His jaw fell open as he gazed at the scene.

Meanwhile the Jeep driver spotted the farmer and his blank stare changed to one of sudden alarm, as though he was caught doing something naughty.

He quickly turned his Jeep around and sped away down the hill, bells jingling and jangling as he rolled over the terrain. We never saw him again.

Everyone's attention turned to the Ford. There it stood in the open field. If it was capable of a human expression, it would have been one of flabbergasted bewilderment.

"Now I've seen everything! How in the world did you manage that?" Serious at first, he exchanged glances with his companion, shook his head, and then they both laughed.

It was a little funny; we were glad he found some humor in it because we thought he would have us arrested.

The farmer faced Richard and me. He expected an answer, but we had no idea how it happened. We didn't think it was possible to achieve, even if you tried.

"Did that Jeep driver do this? You trusted him?" The farmer was now sympathetic, even a little ashamed for having treated us so badly earlier.

"Why didn't you tell me your car was stuck in the mud? I could have helped you."

Richard and I exchanged doubtful glances.

He wasn't a bad guy. Soon, he and his companion set to work to get the old Ford back flat on the ground. They were careful and skilled. It took them some time to decide and implement a plan, but finally we watched silently as they gently brought the car down without any further damage.

They worked a miracle; Richard and I would have never figured it out. Humbled, we stood by as the farmer smiled. He was proud of his accomplishment. We were just glad he wasn't mad at us.

"You got the keys? Let's give it a start."

"The keys are in the ignition." I replied.

He looked inside, and then shook his head in disbelief.

"It's no wonder it wouldn't budge, it's been in park the whole time!"

I felt like one of the three stooges.

"Don't you know it should be in neutral when you push a car?" The farmer sounded like my dad.

"Yeah. I know, but apparently she doesn't." Richard blamed me.

"Well, did you check before pushing it?" The farmer faced me this time.

"No, I left that up to Richard." I responded. Now I blamed him.

Ignoring both of us, the farmer tried to start the engine himself with no luck. The battery was weak. Everyone pushed Blue onto the road.

"Just let it sit awhile and try again in a few minutes. If you pop start it, just be careful going down that hilly road. Don't end up in the ravine." He seemed to care about us.

The farmer and his friend got back in their truck and drove away, leaving Richard and me alone with Blue.

We just stood silently observing the new dents in the old Ford.

After a while, we tried to start the car. The battery was nearly dead. We would have to try our original plan to "pop start" the engine.

We pushed Blue close to an area of the road that began sloping downward. We needed a hill to create momentum. When the car reached a high enough speed, it might start automatically when the ignition was turned. It was our only hope and worth a try.

We both hopped in. This time we made sure the car was in neutral. Because the road was still flat, we had to get it rolling to the slope. Richard held the door open with his leg dangling out pushing the car with his foot. It was kind of like riding a skate board, but old Blue was not a skate board.

When it reached the slope and began barreling downward, Richard quickly flung his leg back in and shut the door.

This was no easy task because he also had to grip the steering wheel to keep the car under control while it rumbled over pot holes.

We soon found ourselves racing down the narrow dirt road. Bordered closely by ditches and deep ravines, trees and thick brush enticed the Ford to swerve in their direction.

We couldn't control the speed of the car and the bumps jostled the wheels making steering difficult. We nearly hit a tree on the left, and then barely missed one on the right.

Braking was close to impossible; instead of slowing down, the tires slid along the damp slick dirt.

It was like a roller coaster ride, but there was no going up, it was all downhill.

Richard looked petrified. He gripped the steering wheel; his knuckles were white and his face was ashen. One foot was hitting the brake pedal and he was concentrating on controlling the car.

The old Ford seemed to gleefully run down the hill like a two year old in a parking lot with his mother chasing him.

The speedometer hit 30 mph. "Start it!" I shouted. Bouncing along, I nearly struck my head on the cloth roof of the old car.

"We're going 30, turn the ignition key!"

Finally, Richard heard me, but the old Ford wouldn't start.

"Keep trying!"

We continued to recklessly speed and swerve with every bump in the road. I hung on for dear life and vowed I would never ride a roller coaster again as long as I lived.

I thought we would crash. Why we didn't, I'll never know, but the old Ford finally started.

With a sudden jerk, it came to life and purred like a kitten. Instantly it became easier to handle.   We were greatly relieved when we were finally on Coast highway on flat land.

As soon as we turned off that rough road, the farmer and his companion pulled alongside my Ford.

"Just wanted to make sure you made it alright!" He waved to us and drove on.

Feeling foolish, we had entirely misjudged the farmer and the hippie in the Jeep based on their age and looks.

I suppose the road to wisdom is similar to the road we just traveled, unpaved and full of pot holes.

17. Gorda Mountain, Big Sur

Richard and I drove along Highway 101 in the Big Sur area south of Monterey, California. We were searching for a commune someone told us about. We noticed a hippie guy hitching a ride along the highway and asked him if he knew of any communes. He pointed the way up to what he called Gorda Mountain.

This was another dirt road on a hill. After our last escapade, we were a bit apprehensive. This road was worse than the last one. I wondered if that was an omen about what we would soon encounter.

Covered with large rough and jagged rocks that protruded from the soil, it was a horrible road.

"We can't get our car up that road!" I protested.

"Of course you can," proclaimed the hippie. "Other people have taken it. I agree it's rough, but it's useable."

After being assured by the hitchhiker, who just happened to live nearby, but didn't offer to help, we turned old Blue off the highway and up the hill.

Believing the risk would be worth it, we were up to the challenge. The long struggle up that hill placed a strain on the engine and Blue heated up and had to be turned off periodically. Inching along, it crept slowly.

We often had to push it through, or remove the larger rocks by hand. We felt like pioneers and the old Ford convertible was our covered wagon.

Finally deciding on a good place to set up our tent, we decided to make a campsite. Unfortunately, it was windy.

Our tent was supported by poles and the wind kept blowing it down. We decided to take a stroll and explore the area to look for any others who might be part of a commune.

All we could find were bits of trash scattered about, but no one was around.

We discovered a clearing within a group of tall trees. It had a kind of altar with various bird feathers, animal bones and unusual stones.

"Looks like some voodoo ritual," I joked.

"Maybe it is." Richard sounded serious. It was creepy.

Some distance away, we discovered a circular structure, much like a primitive hut made from building scraps. It was camouflaged by wild brush and trees.

We felt someone was nearby, but no one responded when we called. Richard didn't like any of it; he was wary the whole time.

"Either they're afraid of us, or we should be afraid of them." Richard mused. "They want nothing to do with us." It was a little eerie.

Going back to struggle with the tent, we were able to secure it, but it wobbled in the wind. Then, the rain began.

It rained so much that water soaked the floor of the tent, and I expected the wind to completely collapse the wobbly structure.

When the rain stopped, the fog was so thick we couldn't see five feet in front of us. We watched it lift gradually. Further up the hill, there was a mysterious campfire overlooking us.

Damp, discouraged and distraught, neither Richard nor I cared to find out to whom it belonged.

We were through with Gorda Mountain and Big Sur. We coasted my dented Ford down that rocky wretched road back to Highway 101.

To our surprise, the hippie hitchhiker who told us to go up that road was waiting below, watching us.

"So, I see you actually made it up that hill." He was smiling.

"Yeah, it wasn't easy though."

"My buddy and I had a bet you wouldn't make it. Most cars break down along the way."

"That's not what you told us before."

The hippie laughed. "Well, I just wanted to see if you could make it. We had fun watching you. I thought we'd have to tow you out of there. We run a towing business."

Richard stared at him coldly.

"Hey, peace brother!" The hippie grinned sarcastically while flashing the "V" symbol with his hand.

"Yeah? Well, peace on you too, brother!" Richard snarled while flashing a different hand gesture, and it didn't mean peace.

My idealism about brotherly love fading, we gladly headed back to sunny Los Angeles.

18. The Commune

When we returned to Hollywood, we met a guy with a couple of girls. They were leaving a record store on Sunset. He was the leader of a commune and offered to give Richard the new album if they could go to his place to listen to it. Richard suspected they wanted something in return. He was right.

Offering a free lunch as well as a free Bob Dylan album, Richard agreed to let him into his humble home on Harold Way. Still curious about communes, I went along with them.

Having guests was unusual for Richard. He trusted very few people. In fact, whenever he left the apartment, he would look out the peep hole to make sure no one was in the hallway. He didn't want anyone to see him leaving for fear he would get "ripped off."

When we got to Richard's apartment, Duke, the commune leader, immediately approached the closet, opened it and looked inside.

Richard later told me the guy was "casing it out" to see what valuables he owned.

The girls laughed about his kitchen being nothing more than a closet with a hot plate and refrigerator. Then they bragged about gathering food from dumpsters behind grocery stores.

"We call it dumpster diving. You can get a lot of great stuff that way."

They could mock Richard's little apartment, but at least he didn't obtain food from a dumpster. Richard would never do that.

Duke told us that if we ever needed anything we should just ask for it.

"I'm driving a new car right now, and all I had to do was ask for it."

"Is that right?" Richard humored the guy, but began to suspect he was some kind of "con artist."

"Yep, you just have to ask people in the right way."

He gave the girls some bills from a large stack he held in his hand to go get lunch for all of us.

"Are there any grocery stores around here?" They asked Richard.

"None with dumpsters," he joked. Everyone laughed.

"There's an Italian deli nearby," he added.

Duke sent the girls to get lunch for everyone. Richard was delighted, he loved sandwiches from the little shop.

After the girls returned, they gave every cent in change back to Duke who counted it carefully. He seemed upset the food cost so much. The girls became quiet.

When his angry face diminished to acceptance, the food was passed to everyone.

After listening to all the songs, Duke gave the brand new album to Richard.

"Now, will you give me your stereo?"

Richard looked at him like he was crazy.

"Why would I want to give you my stereo?"

"Brotherhood and sharing, the hip way. I give you the album; you give me the stereo."

"No, man. You can take it back. I'm not giving you my stereo." Richard seemed annoyed and defensive, even a little angry.

"Just kidding, don't get uptight! Keep your stereo and the album."

After lunch they invited us to their house where we would meet the other commune members. We followed their car in mine.

Duke bought gas for my car, and when we were back on the road again, Richard shared his thoughts about Duke.

"I don't trust him. He wants something from us, but I don't know what yet."

"Richard, you are scaring me. Let's turn around and go back."

"No, don't worry. I won't let anything bad happen to us. Trust me." He assured me, but continued, "I wonder if he's going to go back to my place later and steal my stereo and the album along with it."

When we arrived at their house, several small children were present. Everyone sat in a circle and sang songs. They seemed very happy as they passed around a large carton of ice cream with a spoon inside it.

"Duke has yellow eyes, I think he has Hepatitis. He's eating out of the ice cream carton and the kids are eating off the same spoon! Poor kids are all going to get sick." Richard observed with disgust.

When the carton was given to Richard and me, we just hurriedly passed it on to someone else. If this was what a commune was like, I was greatly disappointed.

Afterwards Richard and I were separated. Duke came to take him away to show him around. That's when the ladies of the commune invited me to sit on one of the few living room chairs. They all brought their sewing projects to show me, embroidering, knitting, etc.

They told me how wonderful life was in the commune and how everyone cared about each other. They were trying to make a good impression. Duke was like the dad and whatever he said was obeyed. They were a large group, and someone had to make the rules.

"Wouldn't you like to live here with us?"

"It sounds interesting," I replied, but thought "absolutely not." I had my own Dad at home making the rules. I surely wouldn't make the trade for this one.

"One of the girls offered to take my black velvet coat to hang in the closet for me. I refused at first, but she took it anyway.

Richard returned and the girls left the room to busy themselves. He told me Duke showed him around and asked him if he wanted to join their commune.

"All you have to do is share everything you have with everyone else. That's what we do, and you'll need to follow my orders because I'm in charge." Richard grimaced as he repeated Duke's words.

"I wouldn't join their commune and take orders from him. I don't know who he thinks he is, but he's not giving me orders!" Richard was ready to leave.

Suddenly, an argument broke out between some of the girls and shouting erupted from the kitchen. A tall mom was upset with a shorter brunette. A blonde haired toddler was crying.

Duke came into the room to settle the matter.

"She spanked my child. If my child needs to be spanked, I'll do it, not her."

Duke's words were law: "That child belongs to everyone. If she thinks he needs a spanking, she can give him one. Those are the rules!"

The tall blonde was visibly upset, but kept silent. Tears were in her eyes as she watched the smug brunette walk away to another room taking the reluctant toddler by his hand.

I wanted to argue in her defense, but I would have been greatly outnumbered. Richard seemed to know what I was thinking and whispered: "stay out of it."

When everyone settled back to normal, we stood ready to leave.

"Could I get my velvet coat?" I asked the girls. None of them seemed to know what I was talking about. No one knew who had taken it. No one could find it in any of the closets.

I told Richard. He requested it for me. Still nothing. Finally, he asked Duke.

"Give her the coat." The leader ordered. It was produced within seconds, but the girl that brought it was pouting.

I put on my coat and Richard and I headed for the door. Two thugs we hadn't seen earlier were standing in front of it. One warned: "You can't leave until Duke says so."

Richard grabbed the door knob defiantly, but it had a dead bolt lock and needed a key. We were locked in their house. Meanwhile, Duke had disappeared upstairs.

Richard did not take this lightly. "Either you open this door or I'll bust through the living room window. We're leaving, one way or another," he warned.

He meant business and began to stir into defense mode. Richard's jaws locked stiffly and I saw the muscles in his arms tense. Huge fists were forming from his large hands and his eyes flared wildly. He somehow seemed taller and larger, as though he was a cat puffing himself out ready for battle.

Not one to reckon with if he felt trapped, Richard would go wild if cornered. He would not go down easily.

The leader casually appeared. "You guys planning to leave?" He asked cordially.

"Yeah, but this guy won't open the door." Richard was no longer a nice guy. "What's up with that? Why can't we leave?"

"Oh, you *can* leave. It's just that he knew I wanted to talk to you before you did, that's all."

Richard listened, but was still tense and suspicious.

"So, we've invited you to join our commune, do you accept?"

"No, thanks, it's not for us." Richard replied, "Can you unlock the door, now? We want to leave."

"Yeah, I'll open the door. You two can go anywhere you like, but we want you to leave your car with us. It's sturdy and runs good. We all like it. I filled the gas tank, now you need to leave the car here."

"I can't do that." Richard replied

"Why not?"

"The car isn't mine to give you." Richard tried to think of a way out, but this was all he could come up with. "It's hers."

Duke's attention was drawn to me. "You can go, but your car stays with us. We need it." His request seemed more like a demand.

"Well, I can't give it to you," I replied flatly.

"Why not?"

"It belongs to my Dad." I lied. "He has the title and would come looking for it. He's a hot headed Italian with lots of rough friends in L.A. He'd cause you a lot of trouble. It wouldn't be worth it." I lied some more.

Duke stared at me in deep thought. It was clear that he was used to having his way.

I heard one of the thugs urge him: "Just take it. Just take it."

The tension was high. Richard looked like he would go ballistic at any moment. I stood there with a blank look. After a seemingly long moment of lingering tense anticipation, Duke gave his orders.

"Open the door and let them go." He casually nodded to the thug blocking our exit.

I heard the other one mutter in disagreement while the door was unbolted. Richard quickly turned the knob, allowing me to leave first. Swiftly, he closed the door behind us, hoping no one would follow.

We hurried to my Ford. I was surprised to find it unlocked. I was sure I had locked it securely.

Richard mumbled that they probably broke into it, and quickly added: "Just floor the gas pedal and don't look back."

Although better communes may have existed, this one shattered my ideals of communal living as a possible superior alternative to the conventional lifestyle.

I came to the conclusion that Flower Children left on their own might just end up like the kids in *Lord of the Flies*. *

* *Lord of the Flies* is a novel by William Golding about a group of boys isolated on an island who try to govern themselves with devastating results.

19. Look Pa, No Brakes!

Dad was a certified brake technician. One day when Richard came to visit in Orange County, he helped my dad replace the brake pads on my 1954 Ford convertible.

"Before you drive to L.A., make sure you refill the brake fluid," Dad told Richard as they were putting tools away; but his mind must have been elsewhere.

We did not refill the brake fluid.

After saying our good-byes, I merged onto the onramp of the Santa Ana Freeway heading north to Los Angeles. It was a sunny day and a pleasant ride until we reached busy traffic in the L.A. area. I was singing along with the radio while Richard dozed off.

Turning along a bend in the road, I noticed traffic ahead was backed up on the freeway. I was driving at a speed of about 60 mph. The vehicles were at a standstill, completely stopped. I began to apply my brakes to slow down.

Nothing. NOTHING!

My heart skipped a beat. "Richard, I have no brakes what should I do?" He popped open a sleepy eye, but soon sat straight up with eyes wide open.

"Get in the other lane!" He warned.

"Which lane?" I asked frantically. All three lanes were full and not one was moving. I kept my foot off the gas pedal and hoped momentum would slow us down, but the speed remained steady.

"What should I do?" My hands gripped the steering wheel.

"I don't know." Richard muttered. He wasn't much help. He clutched the dashboard, attempting to keep himself as far from the windshield as possible.

Those were the days before seat belts and air bags, so there wasn't anything else you could do. Days later I thought of the emergency brake, but I didn't at the time.

The radio continued to blast the tune I had been singing along with, but now it was nerve wracking.

"Marry me, BILL!" * The singer wailed, reaching the loudest point of the song.

I didn't dare remove a hand from the steering wheel to turn off the radio, nor did my eyes cease for a moment from being glued to the scene ahead.

It was all up to me. Richard was frozen. I pumped the brakes, over and over, but the pedal went straight to the floor. What a feeling that was!

Gliding along at a high speed with no brakes and a hundred cars at a dead stop in front of me, I had to think fast.

The only way my car could stop would be to crash it into something, but I didn't want to plow head on into anything! I had to think of something quickly.

*Reference to "The Wedding Bell Blues," by The 5th Dimension, 1969.

All lanes were at a full standstill, drivers were sitting quietly, engines purring. All seemed peaceful and lulling along, until I approached with no brakes.

I clutched the steering wheel unsure what to do next. I noticed space between the lanes where each car stood; maybe I could squeeze my car between the stopped cars. It was the only chance I had, and I took it!

I chose the narrow space between the vehicles in the middle and fast lanes. Both drivers were perfectly still while I plowed in between them. Their cars must have been in park because they barely budged as I slid through.

I avoided crashing head on into the back of the black sedan in the middle lane by turning my car slightly, as though gliding into a parking space -- a very narrow one.

I crunched the sedan's rear left corner with my front right fender. I smashed out his tail light, and then scraped the side of the sedan.

Sitting still in the fast lane was a beat up white work van. I embedded my chrome door handle into its white paint with one long deep groove all along its right side, from back fender to passenger door.

Traffic was still not moving. My car, rolling in as it did, was the only action the other vehicles had seen for a while. It was quite a shocker!

Now, it seemed like the three of us were in parking spaces, very tight parking spaces, sandwiched solidly together with me in the middle like a wedge of cheese!

Those two saved me by forcing my Ford to stop. Fortunately, no one was hurt, not even a whip lash!

The impact was abrupt, but surprisingly smooth. The guy to my left just sat still, looking over at me with a puzzled expression. He was wondering how I just seemed to appear out of nowhere and end up between the designated lanes. He leaned over and calmly rolled down the passenger window.

"You okay? What happened?"

"I'm okay. No brakes. You okay?"

"Yep." He couldn't see the newly added long scar that joined the other previous nicks and scratches. "Hey, can you tell me how bad the damage is? I'm not getting out of my van on this freeway. Just tell me how it looks."

I glanced over at the long scratch and described it to him, offering my insurance information.

"No thanks. I'm glad no one was hurt. Just forget about the damage. I'm in a hurry. Goodbye." He seemed glad when traffic picked up. He shifted his van into drive, and sped away.

The sedan driver and Richard both rolled down their windows and were so close they could have kissed. Of course, neither could open their doors.

I apologized and told him I had no brakes. He was amazed at how little damage resulted from such a serious situation. His car drove fine, just a bent back fender and scratches. My front right side was worse.

His passengers were three Asian businessmen dressed in dark suits in the back seat. They appeared confused, but unharmed.

After the driver translated what happened, they appeared grateful and thanked me for not plowing head on directly into the rear of their car. They were all amazed at my skillful driving ability to squeeze in and maneuver my Ford to "park" it the way I did.

It could have been tragic, everyone agreed. I either drove with the skill of a race car driver, or an angel took over the steering wheel.

I would guess it was the angel.

Peace and Love
To
You!

20. Farewell Flower Children

Every good-bye is followed by a hello. The day finally came when it was time to say farewell to Hollywood and the hippie lifestyle. Our journey had reached its destination and we would take our memories with us.

By the end of 1969, the popularity of hippies in Hollywood had declined. It was the end, but also the beginning. Most moved on to school, careers, marriage, families, or just followed their dreams.

Life is for learning and the sixties were the coming of age years for my generation. Yet, we are still aging children.

To establish a world of love and peace is a worthy goal. Someday it may be achieved when it is clear to mankind that each of us is a Child of God, stardust, and golden.

Maybe at some point in time, or on another plane of existence, we will finally get back to the garden! *

Then again, I've always been an idealist.

* References to "Songs to Aging Children Come," and "Woodstock," by Joni Mitchell, 1969.

About the Author

V.M. Brott, M.Ed. taught English Language Arts for over twenty years. Many of these stories were first told to her high school students. They asked to hear them again and again! She promised to include them in a book someday. This is the book they requested.

Ms. Brott was among a group of teachers chosen from throughout her state to collaborate with researchers and leading experts to design and develop the Common Core State Standards (CCSS) for English Language Arts (ELA) at the secondary level.

Ms. Brott enjoys spending time with her family and many grandchildren. Her favorite authors are O. Henry, Edgar Allan Poe, Charles Dickens, and William Shakespeare.

About this Book

The linked short stories in this book enable the stories to be read individually or as a novel. Discussion questions and activities are included on the following pages.

Book Clubs: You may wish to read the questions and activities before and after each story. Discuss the topics to personally connect with each story. Stimulate conversation by sharing experiences.

Teachers: You may use a topic from one of the discussion questions from each story as a journal writing assignment. This will help students gain a sense of personal connection with the story and spark interest. These questions can be used to activate prior knowledge, as well as enhance comprehension of deeper meanings.

Common Core standards are listed for each set of activities, and for each grade level (6, 7, 8, 9-10, 11-12). The number of the particular standard follows the grade level.

CCSS – Common Core State Standards
ELA – English Language Arts
RL – Reading: Literature
W – Writing
SL – Speaking and Listening
L – Vocabulary Acquisition and Use

For complete information on Common Core State Standards, check with your school district.

Hippies of Hollywood

Discussion and Activities for

Readers and Book Clubs

1 "Shoes," pg. 9

Topic Questions for Discussion

CCSS.ELA-Literacy.SL.6.1; 7.1; 8.1; 9-10.1; 11-12.1; **L.**6.5; 6.5.a; 7.5; 7.5.a; 8.5; 8.5.a; 9-10.5; 11-12.5; 11-12.5.a; **RL**.6.1; 7.1;8.1; 9-10.1; 11-12.1; **RL**.6.4; 7.4; 8.4; 9-10.4; 11-12.4.

1. Why do you think the author changes the font in the middle stanza? Is she trying to convey a message regarding the speaker's life as a young woman of the sixties? What is her message?
2. Who is the speaker in the poem?
3. The speaker wears slippers as an infant and also as a retired grandmother. What message does this convey about life's experiences? Cite text evidence to support inferences.
4. A road is often used as a metaphor for life's journey in poems. The author is using the word "shoes" as a metaphor in this poem. What might the shoes represent in life? What is significant about the various styles worn during stages of the speaker's life?

Activity

What kind of "shoes" would you choose as a metaphor to represent your life currently? How do those "shoes" make you feel? Explain by writing a poem, or decorate shoes illustrating who you are at this point in your life.

2 "An Introduction -- Hello Hollywood," pg. 11

Topic Questions for Discussion
CCSS.ELA-Literacy.**SL**.6.1; 7.1; 8.1; 9-10.1; 11-12.1; **RL**.6.1; 7.1; 8.1; 9-10.1; 11-12.1

1. Why did the narrator enjoy visiting Hollywood? Name a place you would enjoy visiting. Explain your reasons.
2. Compare and contrast your perception of a hippie to the narrator's description.
3. Regarding the hippie generation, the narrator states: "…in some ways we were more innocent than today's generation." From what you know about young people of the sixties, would you agree or disagree with that statement? Explain your answer.

****

3 "Santa Ana Winds," pg. 13

Vocabulary
CCSS.ELA-**L.6**.4; 6.4a; 6.4.c; 6.4.d; **L.7**.4; 7.4.a; 7.4.c; 7.4.d; **L.8**.4;.8.4.a; 8.4.c; 8.4.d; **L.9-10**.4; 9-10.4.a; 9-10.4.c; 9-10.4.d; **L.11-12**.4; 11-12.4.a; 11-12.4.c; 11-12.4.d

Use context clues to determine the meaning of each word, then use a dictionary to verify your preliminary determination of the meaning.

assailant	gruff	anticipate
composure	arrogance	replenish

Topic Questions for Discussion

CCSS.ELA-Literacy.SL.6.1; 7.1; 8.1; 9-10.1; 11-12.1; RL.6.1; 7.1; 8.1; 9-10.1; 11-12.1

1. Have you ever felt out of place in an unfamiliar environment? Describe how you felt, or might have felt, during that experience.
2. Why do you think the narrator made friends with the kids at the psychedelic shop? Have you ever made friends with someone outside your "comfort zone"? Compare the benefits and disadvantages in meeting people who are different from your usual crowd.
3. In your opinion, do you think Lori sent the narrator to a phony address in a dangerous neighborhood on purpose? Explain your answer. Cite text evidence to support inferences.
4. Have you ever been in a frightening situation? Describe how you reacted.
5. At the end of the story, the narrator states that she never said she "hated cops" again. What are the messages the author is conveying about friendship, trust, and carelessness of teenagers?

****

4 "The Doors," pg. 21

Topic Questions for Discussion

CCSS.ELA-Literacy.SL.6.1; 7.1; 8.1; 9-10.1; 11-12.1; L.6.5; 6.5.a; 7.5; 7.5.a; 8.5; 8.5.a; 9-10.5; 11-12.5; 11-12.5.a; RL.6.1; 7.1; 8.1; 9-10.1; 11-12.1; RL.6.1.4; 7.1.4; 8.1.4; 9-10.1.4; 11-12.1.4.

1. The title refers to several "doors" that are mentioned, some are literal (real) and some are used as symbols. In one instance, it is the name for a group of musicians. How is the word "door" used as a metaphor in the story?

2. The door to the sick boy's room is often closed. When it is open, the narrator learns about his condition. This door can be literal as well as a symbol. As a metaphor, how does his door compare to the tide pools in the first paragraph?
3. Have you ever felt uncomfortable around people who try too hard to make you feel welcome? How did you react, or think you would react in such a situation?
4. At the end of the story, the narrator describes the boy as waiting "within the sunset of a cloudless sky." How is the word "sunset" used as a metaphor to describe the boy's situation?
5. The very last sentence hints at the narrator's feelings about life in general. What does her statement infer about life?

Activities: Short Research Projects
CCSS.ELA-Litteracy.W.6.7; 7.7; 8.7; 9-10.7; 11-12.7.

I.   Listen to a recording of "The End" by Jim Morrison. Do you think he was talking about death? Could the lyrics be referring to another kind of ending, such as a friendship or romantic relationship? Explain your answer.
II. What are tide pools and what do they reveal?

5 "The Jimi Hendrix Experience," pg. 29

Topic Questions for Discussion
CCSS.ELA-Literacy.SL.6.1; 7.1; 8.1; 9-10.1; 11-12.1; RL.6.1; 7.1; 8.1; 9-10.1; 11-12.1.

1. How did the concert and the audience reflect the young people of the sixties? Explain. What would you consider a good reflection of today's young adults? Explain.
2. How did the wind and the design of the outdoor amphitheater contribute to the excitement of the audience? How can the environment influence a person's feelings, behavior, and actions? Compare a religious ceremony to that of a concert.
3. The narrator states that her new outlook "drew her like a moth to fire," what do you think she means? Name something that may "draw" young people that might not be a wise choice.

****

6 "Moon Light at Griffith Park," pg. 35

Vocabulary
CCSS.ELA-L.6.4; 6.4a; 6.4.c; 6.4.d; L.7.4; 7.4.a; 7.4.c; 7.4.d; L.8.4; 8.4.a; 8.4.c; 8.4.d; L.9-10.4; 9-10.4.a; 9-10.4.c; 9-10.4.d; L.11-12.4; 11-12.4.a; 11-12.4.c; 11-12.4.d

Use context clues to determine the meaning of each word, then use a dictionary to verify your preliminary determination of the meaning.

insignificant	devotee	radical	disruption
intruder	dominant	medallion	muttering
silhouette	fluttered	sluggish	complacently

Topic Questions for Discussion

CCSS.ELA-Literacy.SL.6.1; 7.1; 8.1; 9-10.1; 11-12.1; **RL**.6.1; 7.1; 8.1; 9-10.1; 11-12.1.

1. Have you ever misjudged someone based on his or her appearance? Were you surprised when you discovered the truth about that person? How did you feel?
2. Do you think the narrator was foolish to go to the park alone? Was it wise to stay in the park while everyone was leaving?
3. Have you ever seen the moon larger than usual? What connotations or feelings does the moon evoke? Why?
4. Compare and contrast the narrator's reaction in this story with her encounter with the man in black in "Santa Ana Winds."
5. At the end of the story, the narrator states that she knew "just who to thank." To whom is she referring? Cite text evidence to support inferences.
6. As angry as she is, why doesn't the narrator ram her car into the little foreign car's back bumper? Why do you think she lets him out of her view in the busy traffic? What would you have done in her situation?

****

7 "Richard the Rogue," pg. 45

Topic Questions for Discussion

CCSS.ELA-Literacy.SL.6.1; 7.1; 8.1; 9-10.1; 11-12.1; **RL**.6.1; 7.1; 8.1; 9-10.1; 11-12.1.

1. Describe Richard as he is introduced in this story.
2. Based on his appearance, attitude, personality, and what you have learned about his life, imagine his childhood. Describe how his past may have influenced who he is now.

3. What is your personal opinion of Richard as a character? Do you think you would like him if you met him? Why or why not?
4. What does the narrator imply, when she describes herself as "naïve?"

Activity: Short Research Project
CCSS.ELA-Literacy.W.6.7; 7.7; 8.7; 9-10.7; 11-12.7.

Using the internet, find a picture taken of the lead singer of "Herman's Hermits" and Mick Jagger during the 1960s. Do you agree with the narrator that one is "baby faced" and the other has a "rugged look?"

****

8 "The Draft Dodger," pg. 49

Topic Questions for Discussion
CCSS.ELA-Literacy.SL.6.1; 7.1; 8.1; 9-10.1; 11-12.1; RL.6.1; 7.1; 8.1; 9-10.1; 11-12.1

1. Although the title refers to Richard, the reader also learns something about the narrator. Describe the narrator's personality and general characteristics based on her actions in this story. Cite text evidence to support inferences.
2. Does the story clearly state the reason why Richard was considered 4-F by the draft board? Although he is never given an explanation, what do you think are some reasons why a person would be considered "not qualified for military service?"

145

Activities: Short Research Projects
CCSS.ELA-Literacy.W .6.7; 7.7; 8.7; 9-10.7; 11-12.7.

I. Using the internet, research The Roxy Hotel in Hollywood, California and describe it as it is today. Find the location on an online map. Richard spent a lot of time on Sunset Boulevard. Using the map, find the address and count how many blocks (or miles) Richard would have to walk to arrive at the corner of Sunset and Vine.

II. Research the consequences of being a draft dodger during the late 1960s. Were many young men sent to jail? Did many young men flee to Canada? What would you have done in their situation?

****

9 "The Cuckoo Clocks," pg. 57

Topic Questions for Discussion
CCSS.ELA-Literacy.SL.6.1; 7.1; 8.1; 9-10.1; 11-12.1; L.6.5; 6.5.a; 7.5; 7.5.a; 8.5; 8.5.a; 9-10.5; 11-12.5; 11-12.5.a; RL.6.1; 7.1; 8.1; 9-10.1; 11-12.1

1. The title refers to the literal cuckoo clocks in the story, but how may they symbolize the characters in the story? Explain by citing text evidence to support inferences.

2. What do you think is meant by the terms "living in the moment" and "cherishing a seemingly crazy, but simple spark in time?" Describe a moment you cherish that was a "seemingly crazy, but simple spark in time."

3. Neither the narrator, nor Richard can understand why the landlady and her husband celebrate each hour. Can

you infer why they celebrate by using clues the author included about the landlady?

4. If possible, using the internet, listen to the songs that the young couple sang at the beginning of the story. Do you think the songs were funny to sing, lighthearted, or romantic?

****

10 "The Elevator Ride," pg. 63

Topic Questions for Discussion

CCSS.ELA-Literacy.SL.6.1; 7.1; 8.1; 9-10.1; 11-12.1; L.6.5; 6.5.a; 7.5; 7.5.a; 8.5; 8.5.a; 9-10.5; 11-12.5; 11-12.5.a; RL.6.1; 7.1; 8.1; 9-10.1; 11-12.1

1. Why did the couple hike all the way up the stairs? Why was the narrator upset with Richard when they reached the top of the hill?

2. Why did the narrator decide to get into the elevator? Describe an experience you have had where you did something against your better judgment. What were the consequences?

3. How are similes, metaphors, and personification used in the story? Find examples of each.

4. How did the residents of the neighborhood initially react when the elevator hit bottom? How did they change when they realized no one was injured from the plunging elevator?

5. Why do you think they were angry when they watched the young people emerge? How do you think their reaction would have differed if it was a nicely dressed older

147

couple? Why?

6. Richard didn't want the narrator to say anything to the stranger as they met him a second time. He also hurried to the busy street. In your opinion, what do you think was his reason for doing so? Explain.

****

11 "Long Beautiful Hair," pg. 71

Vocabulary
CCSS.ELA-L.6.4; 6.4a; 6.4.c;.6.4.d; **L.**7.4; 7.4.a; 7.4.c; 7.4.d; **L.**8.4; 8.4.a; 8.4.c; 8.4.d; **L.**9-10.4; 9-10.4.a; 9-10.4.c; 9-10.4.d; **L.**11-12.4; 11-12.4.a; 11-12.4.c; 11-12.4.d

Use context clues to determine the meaning of each word, then use a dictionary to verify your preliminary determination of the meaning.

euphoric   charlatan

Topic Questions for Discussion
CCSS.ELA-Literacy.SL.6.1; 7.1; 8.1; 9-10.1; 11-12.1; **RL.**6.1; 7.1; 8.1; 9-10.1; 11-12.1

1. Why do you think the audience wanted to believe the narrator and Richard had appeared in the play? Explain.

2. Have you ever watched a movie or play that created an emotional response from you or someone else? Describe the emotional response and what prompted it.

3. What is the inferred message of the story regarding people who are loved by the public, but when they are alone, are forgotten? Cite text evidence to support your answer.

Activity: Short Research Project
CCCSS.ELA-Litteracy.W.6.7; 7.7; 8.7; 9-10.7; 11-12.7.

Research the play and music of *Hair: The American Tribal Love-Rock Musical*. Summarize the public reaction to both.

****

12 "Bel Aire Baloney," pg. 75

Vocabulary
CCSS.ELA-L.6.4; 6.4a; 6.4.c; 6.4.d; **L.**7.4; 7.4.a; 7.4.c; 7.4.d; **L.**8.4; 8.4.a; 8.4.c; 8.4.d; **L.**9-10.4; 9-10.4.a; 9-10.4.c; 9-10.4.d; **L.**11-12.4; 11-12.4.a; 11-12.4.c; 11-12.4.d

Use context clues to determine the meaning of each word, then use a dictionary to verify your preliminary determination of the meaning.

ecstatic   compensation

Topic Questions for Discussion
CCSS.ELA-Literacy.SL.6.1; 7.1; 8.1; 9-10.1; 11-12.1; **L.**6.5; 6.5.a; 7.5; 7.5.a; 8.5; 8.5.a; 9-10.5; 11-12.5; 11-12.5.a; **RL.**6.1; 7.1; 8.1; 9-10.1; 11-12.1

1. How is the word "baloney" used in both a literal and figurative way in the story?

2. Richard developed the "ability to transcend to another reality" using his imagination. Do you think this ability helped him cope through his life's experiences? Explain.

3. Do you agree with the narrator's mother that "poor people have something the rich want," or is it the other way around, in your opinion? What could poor people possibly

have that money couldn't buy? Explain.

4. According to Richard, why didn't he tell the wealthy couple he wanted to quit? Why do you think he enjoyed the care and attention he received from the couple?

5. In your opinion, was the wealthy couple more concerned about Richard, a possible lawsuit, or both? Explain your answer by citing text evidence to support inferences.

6. The narrator calls the guitar an "ego trip," what does she infer about both the guitar and the mansion in Bel Aire?

Activity: Short Research Project
CCCSS.ELA-Litteracy.W.6.7; 7.7; 8.7; 9-10.7; 11-12.7.

A famous suspense writer (popular during the sixties) is mentioned in the story. According to the clues in the story, can you guess who he might have been? (Clue: he is known not only for suspense, but also for **psycho**logical thrillers.) Find a picture of him. Are his movies still shown on television?

****

13 "The Cookie Guy," pg. 87

Topic Questions for Discussion
CCSS.ELA-Literacy.SL.6.1; 7.1; 8.1; 9-10.1; 11-12.1; RL.6.1; 7.1; 8.1; 9-10.1; 11-12.1

1. What is the message of the story regarding hard work and lots of effort? Cite text evidence to support inferences.

Activity: Short Research Project

CCCSS.ELA-Litteracy.W.6.7; 7.7; 8.7; 9-10.7; 11-12.7.

Can you guess the name of the cookie maker? The narrator implies that the cookies are sold in grocery stores. However, the packages no longer resemble lunch bags and the "cookie guy" is no longer pictured. Try to find chocolate chip cookies that may have been produced by someone who became "**famous**" (clue). You may want to research the history of the company. Was the company founded by someone in the Los Angeles area during the 1960s or 1970s? If yes, it may be the "cookie guy" from the story.

****

14 "The Celebrities," pg. 91

Topic Questions for Discussion

CCSS.ELA-Literacy.SL.6.1; 7.1; 8.1; 9-10.1; 11-12.1; L.6.5; 6.5.a; 7.5; 7.5.a; 8.5; 8.5.a; 9-10.5; 11-12.5; 11-12.5.a; RL.6.1; 7.1; 8.1; 9-10.1; 11-12.1

1. What is the narrator implying about the similarities and differences between celebrities and common people? Cite text evidence to support inferences.

2. Define the word "illusion." How can the Hollywood sign, movies, and a Rolls Royce limousine be considered illusions?

3. What is your opinion of the chauffeur/writer in the story? In your opinion, does he seem lonely, unhappy, or disillusioned? Cite an example that

would support your answer.

4. Contrast the differences between Richard and the narrator's thoughts concerning fame.

Activities: Short Research Projects
CCSS.ELA-Litteracy.W.6.7; 7.7; 8.7; 9-10.7; 11-12.7.

I. Find a copy of Emily Dickinson's poem ("I'm Nobody! Who are you?"). If you were in the limo, would you have enjoyed the illusion of the ride? Write a poem similar to Dickinson's from the point of view of a popular celebrity. You may begin with the words: "I'm Somebody! Who are you?"

II. Richard worked as an extra in a Western musical that needed many young men as extras. It was produced in the late 1960s and had a gold mining theme. Research to find the possible title of the movie. You might be able to view it on You Tube, and actually see Richard in one of the saloon scenes (if you're patient and observant).

****

15 "A Case of Mistaken Identity," pg. 99

Topic Questions for Discussion
CCSS.ELA-Literacy.SL.6.1; 7.1; 8.1; 9-10.1; 11-12.1; RL.6.1; 7.1; 8.1; 9-10.1; 11-12.1

1. The narrator compares real life with the action, adventure, surprise and drama of the movies. Compare a moment in your own life with a scene

from a movie. Describe it in a short essay.

2. What made the young couple believe the two men at the door were plain clothes police officers? What made the two men think Freddie was behind the locked door? Cite text evidence to support inferences.

3. In your opinion, should the narrator have told Richard about the gun hidden in the man's pocket while they talked to him? How do you think the two men would have reacted if she did?

4. After Richard realizes their lives had been in danger, he does not want to listen to a song about guns. Have you ever had a negative experience that you wanted to forget? Explain.

Activity: Short Research Project
CCSS.ELA-Litteracy.W.6.7; 7.7; 8.7; 9-10.7; 11-12.7.

Listen to the three recordings mentioned in the story from the Beatles "White Album." After hearing them, do you think they would have added suspense to the story? Why?

****

16 "Going up the Country," 107

Topic Questions for Discussion
CCSS.ELA-Litteracy.SL.6.1; 7.1; 8.1; 9-10.1; 11-12.1; **L**.6.5; 6.5.a; 7.5; 7.5.a; 8.5; 8.5.a; 9-10.5; 11-12.5; 11-12.5.a; **RL**.6.1; 7.1; 8.1; 9-10.1; 11-12.1.

1. At the beginning of the story, the narrator states that her dad often told her she had a lot to learn. What did she learn by the end of the story?

2. Why did the young couple trust the hippie in the jeep? Would you have trusted him? Why, or why not?

3. Have you ever witnessed an unusual occurrence that you didn't think was possible? Explain.

4. What would have been a wiser solution to get the car started and out of the mud? What does their problem solving ideas indicate about the young couple?

5. Do you agree with the narrator's metaphor about the road to wisdom being unpaved and full of pot holes? Why or why not? Explain.

****

17 "Gorda Mountain, Big Sur," pg. 117

Vocabulary
CCSS.ELA-L.6.4; 6.4a; 6.4.c; 6.4.d; **L.7.4**; 7.4.a; 7.4.c; 7.4.d; **L.8.4**; 8.4.a; 8.4.c; 8.4.d; **L.9-10.4**; 9-10.4.a; 9-10.4.c; 9-10.4.d; **L.11-12.4**; 11-12.4.a; 11-12.4.c; 11-12.4.d

Use context clues to determine the meaning of each word, then use a dictionary to verify your preliminary determination of the meaning.

distraught   sarcastic   wretched   idealism   omen.

Topic Questions for Group Discussion
CCSS.ELA-Literacy.SL.6.1; 7.1; 8.1; 9-10.1; 11-12.1; RL.6.1; 7.1; 8.1; 9-10.1; 11-12.1

1. Which sentence is an example of foreshadowing in the second paragraph at the beginning of the story?

2. What is a commune? Why does the narrator want to visit one of them?

3. Have you ever looked forward to an adventure that turned out to be a miserable experience? Summarize with a brief description.

4. Why was Richard angry with the hippie who was watching as they drove down the hill? Cite text evidence to support inferences.

****

18 "The Commune," pg. 121

Topic Questions for Discussion
CCSS.ELA-Literacy.SL.6.1; 7.1; 8.1; 9-10.1; 11-12.1; RL.6.1; 7.1; 8.1; 9-10.1; 11-12.1

1. Describe Duke, the commune leader. In your opinion, was he a good leader? Why or why not?

2. Why didn't Richard trust Duke? In your opinion, why did Richard continue to associate with Duke?

3. At the beginning of the story, Richard suspects that

Duke wants something in return, what did he want?

4. Do you think the girls in the commune were purposefully being deceitful about it, or do you think they were truly happy following Duke's rules? Explain your answer.

5. When Duke explains that whenever he wants something, all he has to do is ask for it. Richard thinks he's a "con artist." What does he mean by that term?

6. Why would "dumpster diving" be prohibited by stores?

7. Do you think you would enjoy living in the commune described in the story? Why or why not?

8. Duke tried to get the narrator's car in at least two ways, describe them.

9. Do you think the young couple was in danger when they discovered they had been locked in the house? What do you think the thug was suggesting when he urged Duke to "just take it"?

10. In your opinion, why did Duke let the couple leave with their car? Cite text evidence to support inferences.

Activities: Short Research Projects
CCSS.ELA-Litteracy.W.6.7; 7.7; 8.7; 9-10.7; 11-12.7.

I.   Research Hepatitis. Are one of its symptoms yellow eyes? Can you contract the disease by sharing food from the same spoon?

II. Read a summary of the book *Lord of the Flies*. How do the boys and the story itself compare to the commune?

****

19 **"Look Pa, No Brakes!" pg. 129**

Topic Questions for Discussion
CCSS.ELA-Literacy.SL.6.1; 7.1; 8.1; 9-10.1; 11-12.1; **RL**.6.1; 7.1; 8.1; 9-10.1; 11-12.1

1. Why wasn't the Ford able to stop? Who was to blame?

2. Why do you think the driver of the van didn't want to wait to exchange insurance information after the accident?

3. Although the story is based on a true event, do you think it would have been impossible to occur without more serious results? Explain.

4. Consider the narrator's experiences in "Moonlight at Griffith Park," and "The Elevator Ride," as well as in this story. Do these stories infer that the narrator had spiritual faith? Cite text examples to support inferences.

Activity: Short Research Project
CCSS.ELA-Litteracy.W.6.7; 7.7; 8.7; 9-10.7; 11-12.7.

Listen to a recording of "The Wedding Bell Blues." Imagine yourself as a passenger in the front seat of the narrator's Ford when the singer becomes loudest. Write a short narrative essay about what you would be thinking and feeling at that moment.

****

20. "Farewell Flower Children," pg. 135

Topic Questions for Discussion
CCSS.ELA-Literacy.SL.6.1; 7.1; 8.1; 9-10.1; 11-12.1; **RL**.6.1; 7.1; 8.1; 9-10.1; 11-12.1; **RL**.6.4; 7.4; 8.4; 9-10.4; 11-12.4.

1. What is the deeper meaning inferred by the narrator in the last three paragraphs? To what "garden" is she referring? How can each of us be a child of God, stardust, and golden?

Activity: Short Research Project
CCSS.ELA-Litteracy.W.6.7; 7.7; 8.7; 9-10.7; 11-12.7.

Listen to the songs mentioned in the footnotes. Do the lyrics help with your understanding of the narrator's last three paragraphs? Explain your answer.

****

Final Topic Questions for Discussion

CSS.ELA-Literacy.RL.6.2; 6.3; 7.2; 7.3; 8.2; 8.3; 9-10.2; 9-10.3; 11-12.2; 11-12.3.

1. Determine the theme or central idea of the book as a whole. How is the theme conveyed through particular details? Summarize the book according to the text, without

your personal opinions or judgments.

2. Analyze how the main character developed through the series of episodes over the course of the text. How did she change or respond as the stories moved toward the final resolution in "Farewell Flower Children"? How did the main character advance the plot to develop the theme of the book as a whole?

3. The author never reveals the name of the narrator. Why do you think she left her nameless? What is the name you would have given her, and why?

4. Complete a short character sketch for each one, the narrator and Richard.

5. Draw a Venn diagram, use it to compare and contrast the narrator and Richard. Include details on how they are alike, and how they are different.

6. Write a short essay on what you have learned about the 1960s and hippies.

7. Are there still hippies in the world today? Explain.

8. The narrator does not tell the reader what happened after the couple left the hippie scene of Hollywood. As a result, the reader may feel that the story had no ending. Create an ending for both the narrator and Richard and where they might be today. Did they go separate ways, or stay together? If they were 20 years old in 1968, how old would they be today?

Final Narrative Writing Project

CCSS.ELA-Literacy.W.6.3; 7.3; 8.3; 9-10.3; 11-12.3; W.6.3.d; 7.3.d; 8.3.d; 9-10; 11-12.d;.W.6.3.e; 7.3.e; 8.3.e; 9-10.e; 11-12.e.

The stories in this book are narratives. Whenever you tell a story from the first person point of view about something you did or an event in your life, it is considered a narrative.

The author uses the basic plot structure in many of her narratives. List the five elements of a plot (introduction, rising action, climax, falling action, and resolution) to analyze the plot structure of "Santa Ana Winds."

The climax would be at the moment the narrator is hiding on the old man's porch and hears her assailant's footsteps nearby. Knowing this is the climax, what could you tell about the other elements of the plot in the story?

To write your own narrative, first outline a plot structure. Be sure to include the five elements. Similar to a five paragraph essay, you would begin with an introduction.

Be sure to include well-chosen details, well-structured event sequences, and sensory language to convey vivid pictures of the experience, event, setting and characters. Also, use transition words, phrases and clauses to convey sequence and signal shifts from one time frame or setting to another.

End your narrative with a conclusion that follows from and reflects on what is experienced, observed, or resolved over the course of the narrative. This would be the resolution in your plot structure.

If you can tell about an experience, you can write about it! Just try it and you'll see! Write on!

www.ingramcontent.com/pod-product-compliance
Lightning Source LLC
Chambersburg PA
CBHW070928130626
46555CB00001B/341